DANNY ORLIS
BIG BROTHER

DANNY ORLIS BIG BROTHER

BERNARD PALMER

Danny Orlis Big Brother
© 2023 by Bernard Palmer
All rights reserved. First edition 1959.
Second edition 2024.

Cover image: Adobe Firefly
Character illustrations: John Ball
Editor: Jon D. Fogdall

Aneko Press Youth

www.anekopress.com

Aneko Press, Life Sentence Publishing, and our logos are trademarks of Life Sentence Publishing, Inc.
203 E. Birch Street
P.O. Box 652
Abbotsford, WI 54405

JUVENILE FICTION / Religious / Christian / Action & Adventure
Paperback ISBN: 978-1-62245-982-7
eBook ISBN: 978-1-62245-983-4
10 9 8 7 6 5 4 3 2 1
Available where books are sold

CONTENTS

CHAPTER 1

NEW FRIENDS

The time had come for Danny Orlis and the twins, Ron and Roxie, to go back to school at Cedarton, Minnesota. They left Angle Inlet on the little mail boat and went down to Warroad where they were to take the bus.

"You'll look after the twins, won't you, Danny?" Mrs. Orlis had asked apprehensively.

"Sure, I will."

"It's going to be harder for them now that they're in high school," she continued. "There'll be so many problems that they've never faced before."

"Don't worry about Ron and Roxie, Mother," Danny told her. "They're going to be all right. Mr. and Mrs. Meyer will look after them the same way you and Dad do at home."

"That's what I've been trying to tell her, Danny," his dad put in, "but you know how mothers are."

The little boat pulled away from the dock and the twins stood with Danny in the fantail, waving until they left Pine Creek and turned in a wide arc toward American Point.

"I wish Mother wouldn't worry so much about us," Roxie said. "It makes me feel as though she doesn't trust us."

"It's not that at all," her oldest brother said.

"If she doesn't trust you," Ron said, grinning impishly, "she's sure got a good reason for it."

"Ron!" his twin exploded.

* * *

When the bus pulled into Cedarton, Marilyn, Tim, and Kay were waiting at the depot. Kay looked up at the young woodsman.

"Are you surprised to see me here?" she asked.

Danny grinned down at her. "It's a mighty good surprise," he continued, "but to tell you the truth, Dad was over at the Bible Camp the other day and he heard that you were going to school after all."

Tim picked up one of the heavy bags, and Marilyn and Kay helped Roxie with the lighter ones.

* * *

School started for Ron and Roxie Orlis the following morning. They got up early and walked together to the big, brick high school.

"I–I'm scared," Roxie said.

"There isn't anything to be scared of." Ron laughed nervously.

"It was bad enough coming here in the middle of the semester last year, but this is worse. We're going to high school now."

As soon as they registered, the other kids took them in. Roxie remembered some of them, but there were so many new faces, and everybody was hurrying about so much that her head was spinning. A girl her own age came up and asked her to share a locker with her.

"I'm Susan Cain," she said, smiling warmly.

"I–I–."

"Come on," Susan said, taking her by the arm. "If we don't hurry, all the good lockers will be gone."

Susan was about Roxie's height but had flaxen hair and an expensive-looking dress. She was popular too, probably as popular as anyone else in school. Roxie could tell that by the way the other kids turned and spoke to her as they walked along the hall.

The school session was short that day, and they were out before noon.

"Well," Ron asked, grinning, "how did it go, Roxie?"

"Oh, it was wonderful! The kids are so friendly. We're going to have a lot of fun this year."

Susan came running across the street to catch up with them.

"I almost forgot to tell you about the school party,

Roxie," she said excitedly. "You'll be going, won't you?" She looked at Ron.

"I don't know," Ron said. "I haven't heard anything about it."

"Oh, you'll have to go! Besides, this is something new. The Student Council is sponsoring an all-school party, so we can get acquainted with the kids in other classes."

"It sounds like fun," Roxie put in.

"And, Roxie, all the girls wear their new sweaters and skirts in the school colors. Every girl who is anybody at school is in crimson and white."

Roxie's face fell. Her parents hadn't been able to buy her many new clothes this year. She didn't have a sweater and skirt in crimson and white!

"I'll see you in the morning, Roxie," the girl added.

Susan Cain left the twins then and hurried up the street toward the large white house where she lived with her parents.

When she was gone Roxie turned to her twin brother. "Did you hear what she said about the party?"

"Sure. It sounds like a lot of fun."

"That isn't what I mean. All the girls will be wearing crimson and white skirts and sweaters."

Ron looked at her strangely. "So what?"

"But don't you see? I don't have any."

Ron was unimpressed. "What difference does that make?" he asked her.

"The other girls will be in their sweaters and skirts, and I won't." Tears were filling her eyes. "I'm not going, Ron."

They walked on for a block in silence.

"Ron," she said at last in a small voice, "do you suppose if I wrote to Mother and Dad right away that they'd buy me a new sweater and skirt?"

He stopped and turned to face her.

"You can't do that. Our parents have all they can do to keep the three of us in school this winter. We can't expect them to buy things we don't really need."

Roxie was crestfallen. "But I do need them, Ron. You just don't understand. All the girls who are anything at school will be dressed in the school colors. Susan said so."

"Well, it wouldn't worry me."

The following morning Ron reported for Physical Education class. Coach Hanson was the Freshman instructor. He had been assistant coach last year.

"We're going to have a little session of touch football," the coach said as the class of gangling ninth-graders lined up before him. "I want to see what you guys can do. Maybe we can get some new recruits for the second team."

Ron Orlis had never played football before, except with Danny and Jim and a few others up at the Angle. He took his place in the line, and when the ball was snapped, he darted forward.

Coach Hanson spotted him almost instantly.

"You, Orlis," he called, "come here."

Ron went over to him.

"I want to see you run. When I say 'Go,' give it everything you've got for about a hundred yards."

Ron crouched and when the coach shouted, "Go," he blasted at top speed along the track.

"You're pretty fast, aren't you?" the coach asked when Ron came back.

"I like to run."

"Have you ever played football?"

"We played a little sandlot ball up at the Angle," Ron explained, "but that's all."

"Get over there in the backfield, and let's see you handle the ball," the coach ordered.

When the class was over Mr. Hanson approached him.

"You know, Ron," he said, "you've got speed, and for a guy who's never played the game, you handle the ball very well. Why aren't you out for the team?"

"I–I don't know," Ron answered. "I've never cared much for football."

Coach Hanson frowned. "You'd better think it over. We need a guy like you."

Ron walked slowly back to the school to get dressed.

"I heard what Coach Hanson said," Kirk Meyer exclaimed, hurrying up to Ron. "You'll be out for the team tonight, won't you?"

Ron shook his head.

"I'm not sure I want to play football."

"You're not sure you want to play!" Kirk echoed. "But you've got to. Why there isn't another ninth-grader who can run as fast as you can. We've got to have you."

CHAPTER 2

A WISH GRANTED

Ron had asked Roxie not to say anything to Danny about the skirt and sweater she wanted so desperately.

"He's got enough to think about."

However, when Danny came home from Bible school, he found Roxie sitting alone in the living room, a frown on her face.

"Hi, Roxie! How did it go today?"

"All right, I guess," she tried hard to smile.

He went over and sat down beside her. "What do you mean, all right?"

"Everything went fine, Danny," she repeated.

But he wasn't satisfied.

"You don't act as though everything went fine," he said.

She sniffled a little.

"Ron didn't want me to say anything to you about it."

"What's a big brother for if you can't talk to him?" Danny asked. "Tell me all about it."

"You–you'll probably laugh at me the way Ron did. He said I was silly."

Slowly, hesitantly, she told him about the school party, and the fact that all the other girls were going to wear crimson and white outfits.

"Susan says that just about everybody at school will have them," Roxie went on. "She says that the girls dressed in school colors are more apt to be picked for the pep club. They only choose four out of the whole freshman class, and Danny, I'll just die if I don't get to be one of them."

He put his arm about her shoulder awkwardly. "Now you just take it easy, Roxie. We'll see what we can do."

That night Danny talked with Kay about getting Roxie a skirt and sweater.

"I know those things mean an awful lot," she admitted. "That was one of the hard things for me when I was going to high school. Mother couldn't afford to buy me nice clothes like Marilyn and some of the other girls had. There were times when I felt that I couldn't go to parties, or anywhere else where those girls would be."

Danny bit his lower lip. "What would a skirt and sweater cost?"

"I don't know," Kay answered. "I didn't have a skirt and sweater. But I'm sure they'll cost $25.00 or $30.00."

Danny whistled in amazement.

"What were you thinking of?"

"Oh, I was just wondering–." His voice trailed away.

"Wondering how you could get a skirt and sweater for Roxie?" Kay asked him.

"I guess so. It's hard on a kid her age to have to be different than all the others," Danny said.

"There will be a lot of girls in regular dresses at the party," Kay told him. "There always have been. Everyone won't be wearing crimson and white sweaters and skirts. And anyway, Danny, I–I'm not too sure that pep club here at Cedarton is good for her."

"I was thinking the same thing, Kay," Danny replied. "I don't suppose there is anything wrong with the pep club itself, but it's the thing it leads to."

Kay looked up at him, "And the friends she will make there," she said softly. "I think Roxie should concentrate on making Christian friends and going to places like Bible club and Young People's. I remember how pep club conflicted with prayer meeting and church activities last year."

"The more I think of it, the more I think I should discourage her from joining pep club. But Roxie's not the kind of girl you can talk out of something. It's got to be proved to her."

Kay hesitated. "I realize it isn't any of my business,

but I know your parents don't have money to buy everything she wants or thinks she needs. And you should use your money for Bible school. Not for something like this."

Danny was quiet for a long while. "I'm not for this thing either," he said finally. "But somehow, I feel I should get Roxie a sweater and a skirt. I think it will help to prove my point. And while it might cost me something, maybe it will teach Roxie a lesson. Would you go with me and help pick them out?"

Danny and Kay got the sweater and skirt the following afternoon after school, and Danny brought them home. Roxie was in her room studying.

"Hi, Roxie!" he called. "Come here a minute."

A moment later she came down the stairs.

"Are you all set for the party next week?"

"I'm not going." Her lower lip curled slightly.

"Why not?" he asked.

"I'm not going to be laughed at," she said firmly. "I'll stay home."

"Oh, I wouldn't do that if I were you!" With that he put the package in her hand.

"What–what–." She felt that it was soft, and her voice choked off suddenly.

"Danny!" she gasped.

"Well," he said, "go ahead and open it."

"Danny! You didn't!"

Hurriedly she tore open the package, squealing with delight.

"You got me a sweater and skirt!"

"I couldn't have you miss out on the party, now could I?" he asked her.

She held up the sweater and looked at it, beaming.

"Oh, Danny, it's the most beautiful gift I've ever had!"

She ran to a mirror and holding the sweater against her shoulders, she posed happily. "It's the nicest sweater any girl ever had!"

When Ron came home shortly before supper, Roxie was dressed in her new skirt and sweater.

"Where did you get those?" he asked unappreciatively.

"Danny got them for me." She was still trembling with excitement. "I didn't ask him for them, Ron. He just got them for me."

Ron went over to a chair and plopped down on it.

"Do you mean to tell me that Danny took money he had saved to go to Bible school and bought you that outfit?" he asked. "And you took it?"

"But I didn't ask him for it. Honestly, I didn't," she protested.

Ron grunted in disgust. "I'll bet you didn't," he snorted.

CHAPTER 3

UNEXPECTED ENTERTAINMENT

Ron Orlis got acquainted with the boy who sat across from him in his English class. He was a short, stocky guy with a round face and big brown eyes. He was new in school too, and as soon as he heard where Ron was from, he came over to him.

"I'm Dick Masters," he said. "Do you really live up on the Northwest Angle?"

Ron nodded, smiling.

"What's it like?"

"It would take a month to tell you," Ron said loyally, "but it's the finest place on earth."

"Ever trap?"

"Do I! That was one thing I hated most about coming down here to school. I had a swell trap line up on the Angle. Caught a lot of muskrat and a few beaver and mink."

They walked down the long corridor together.

"You know, we should get together," Dick suggested. "I've got about 25 traps. A couple of us should be able to run at least 50."

"I'll write to Dad and have him send my traps down," the boy from the Angle answered.

"Swell." Dick was grinning broadly. "I've got a place for the trap line all picked out and everything."

Ron Orlis was tingling with excitement. He could scarcely wait to get home and tell Roxie and Danny what had happened.

"But you aren't going to do it, are you?" Roxie asked.

"A guy doesn't get a chance like this every day."

"But what about football and hockey and basketball? If you're fiddling around with those traps, you won't have time to go out for sports."

"There's enough sport in running a trap line to suit me," he said.

"But, Ron," Roxie protested, "I already told all the kids that you were going out for football."

"There's nothing to it," Ron said. "I'll just tell them that I'm not."

He learned, however, that it wasn't as easy to keep from playing football as he had thought. Kirk and two other guys came to talk to him the next morning before school, and at noon Coach Hanson sought him out.

"We haven't seen you out for football yet, Orlis," he said.

Ron felt his cheeks flush. "I haven't decided whether I want to play or not."

"We really need you. We might even be able to use your speed on the first team toward the end of the season."

* * *

"I just don't know what to do, Danny," Ron confided that evening when the two of them sat alone together.

"Dick and I have our trap line all set up. I can earn some extra money and help out by buying my own clothes and have spending money too. I don't think I care to go out for football."

"Then I wouldn't go out," Danny answered. "I played when I was in high school, and I enjoyed every minute of it. But I know that any money you can make with a trap line will help a lot. It's quite a burden for our parents to have the three of us living away from home and going to school."

Ron smiled. "You seem to have an answer for everything, Danny."

His older brother shook his head.

"All I can do is to tell you what I learned by making mistakes, Ron," he said.

"Danny," Ron said impulsively, "I want to be just like you when I grow up."

Danny Orlis' face clouded. "You'd better not say that, Ron. If you try to follow me, you'll only be disappointed. Don't model your life after anyone. Go to the Bible and model your life after the Lord Jesus. He's the only One who is completely safe to follow."

The next morning Danny was up early and went across town toward the Cedarton Bible Institute. As he walked by the bus depot a voice hailed him.

"Hey, guy!" a strangely familiar voice called to him from across the street. "Can you tell me if there happens to be a Bible school here?"

"Why, Chuck Martin!" the young woodsman exclaimed. "What are you doing here?"

Grinning, Chuck set down his bags to shake hands with Danny. "It's a long story, but I finally decided that I'd better come up here to school after all."

"Fine," Danny said. "I know you'll like it. Come on, I'll help you with those bags."

As they walked along together, Chuck told him how he had fought attending a Bible Institute, and how he had gone back to his former school and had registered.

"I even went to classes for a couple of days," Chuck said. "But all the while I felt that I wasn't doing the right thing. There was so much there that wasn't Christian, I began to feel the need, more and more, of getting into a place where I could get some good sound Bible training. So, finally I called Dr. Nielsen, and here I am."

"That's swell."

"How's Kay?" Chuck asked abruptly. "She was able to enroll here all right, wasn't she?"

Danny turned quickly to look at him. Was it because of Kay that Chuck had come to Cedarton?

"She's fine," Danny said, struggling to keep the edge out of his voice. "She's staying at Marilyn's and going to school. The Foresters have taken on her support."

"Her faith certainly taught me a lesson. I don't think I'd be here this morning if it hadn't been for her and the way she faced the fact that she might not get to school at all."

* * *

For several days, the whole high school had been buzzing with excitement about the coming party. It was to be held in the school gymnasium and everybody was invited.

"What's the party going to be like?" Ron asked Kirk as they got ready that evening. "Everybody is talking about how wonderful it's going to be, but nobody knows much about it."

"It's supposed to be a surprise," Kirk said. "The Student Council got it up. They don't want anybody to know until we get there."

Roxie came tripping down the stairs, her small face beaming. "Oh, Ron," she thrilled, "aren't this skirt and sweater beautiful?"

"They should be," he said. "Danny took money he had saved for Bible school to buy them for you."

Her face darkened momentarily.

"Don't keep reminding me of that, or I won't be able to enjoy wearing them."

The big gymnasium was almost filled with kids by the time the twins and Kirk and Karen arrived. Ron stood in the doorway and looked about.

"Look, Roxie!" he said softly. "There are a lot of girls here who aren't in outfits like you made Danny buy for you."

She made a little face at him and moved away.

Although most of the kids were already there, the party didn't start immediately. Ron sought out Dick Masters to talk to him about their trap line. They were standing together in one corner, away from the other kids, when the orchestra began to play. Ron looked up.

"What's going on?" he asked.

"I don't know," Dick said. "Looks to me as though they're going to dance."

The students began to move off the floor to make room for the few who were beginning, self-consciously, to dance to the music of the high school orchestra.

"I didn't know this was going to be a dance," Ron said. "Why didn't you tell me, Dick?"

"I didn't know it either. But what's the difference?"

Ron did not answer him. Roxie was standing with Susan and three other girls across the way.

"I'll see you tomorrow, Dick," Ron said, moving toward his sister.

She saw him coming and walked rapidly away from her friends to meet him.

"Roxie," he said, "I think we should go home."

"But, why?" she asked, lowering her voice and looking about to see whether anyone heard him. "We just got here."

"This isn't any place for us. They're going to dance all evening."

"But what will the other girls think if I leave?" she protested.

"Who cares what they think?"

She looked back toward Susan and the little group of girls around her. Susan smiled and motioned to her.

"I'm not going to dance, Ron," she said. "I was just standing there talking. There isn't any harm in that."

"The Bible tells us that we're to stay away from the very appearance of evil," he reminded her. "You know what Danny and our parents and our church think about dancing. They can't all be wrong."

Roxie's lips began to tremble. "You just want to spoil all the good times I have, Ron Orlis!"

CHAPTER 4

STILL CONTRARY

For a moment or two Ron Orlis stood before Roxie.

"We don't want to stay," he said. "Think of what it will do to our testimony."

"But I'm not going to dance, Ron," Roxie answered petulantly. "I was just getting acquainted with some of the kids."

"You can get acquainted with them some other time."

The corners of Roxie's lips pulled down into a pout.

The music stopped and everybody clapped as the floor cleared.

"If we've got to go, Ron," she spoke quickly, "let's go now so they won't see us."

She tried to slink away into the crowd, but Susan spotted her.

"Where are you going, Roxie?" her new friend called out.

The color came up into the girl's cheeks. "I'll see you tomorrow."

"The party's just getting started."

Without answering, Roxie turned and pushed her way to the door and hurried outside. Ron followed.

"I don't see why we couldn't stay and watch for a little while," she said curtly as they went out into the chill October air. "What are the kids going to think?"

"What do we care?" Then he stopped and turned to face her. "You know, Roxie," he said, his voice growing soft, "Danny warned us about this. He said we were going to have to make all sorts of decisions. Some of the kids are going to laugh at us if we stand up for what we believe, but we can't let that bother us."

"I know," her voice small and weak.

"Besides, the kids will respect us more if we do stand up for what we believe. Danny was telling me some of the troubles he had when he first went to Iron Mountain to school. And even when he came here to Cedarton. He found out that the kids who razzed him the most actually respected him when they learned that he had backbone enough to stand up for what he believed."

Ron was silent for a moment. "That's the way it can be with you and me," he continued. "We haven't got it nearly as hard as Danny had it. He had to stand alone. We've got him and Kirk and Karen, and each other."

"I still don't see that it would have hurt if we'd stayed at the gym for a little while tonight."

The next day at school Ron took a great deal of good-natured kidding because he left the party.

"What happened last night?" Dick Masters asked. "Were you afraid that someone would make you dance with a girl?"

"Nope," he grinned. And then his face grew serious. "I couldn't stay at the dance, Dick. I'm a Christian, and I feel that it's best for a Christian not to do those things. To tell you the truth, if I had known that it was going to be a dance I wouldn't even have gone."

Dick looked at him oddly. "Boy, you are religious, aren't you?"

"I wouldn't say that a guy was too religious just because he didn't do something he felt was wrong, would you?" Ron asked him. "The Bible tells us that we should separate ourselves from the world."

"I was just asking you. I didn't expect a sermon."

The girls gathered around Roxie that morning. "What happened to you last night?" Susan asked her." I wanted to introduce you to some of the girls in the pep club. But when I looked up there you were going out the door."

Roxie flushed.

"Ron thought we'd better go home."

"You don't have to mind him, do you?" Then, before Roxie could answer, she took her by the arm. "Come on, we've just got time to go down the hall. I want you to meet Mary and JoJo. They're the ones you have to know if you expect to get into the pep club."

During the Physical Education class the coach insisted on keeping Ron in the backfield. He taught him how to take a pass from center and how to throw his hips to avoid a would-be tackler.

"You come by the stuff naturally, Orlis," he said. "I'd give anything if we could talk you into playing football."

"Football?" one of the other guys echoed. "You don't expect him to play football, do you, Coach? Why, he won't even dance."

Ron bit his lower lip but said nothing.

* * *

Kay Milbourn enjoyed her new room very much. Mrs. Forester had insisted that she take the one across from Marilyn's room.

"I want you girls to be close together," the older woman explained. "It's so good to have a fine Christian girl in the house to be a companion to Marilyn."

"You'll never know how much I appreciate it, Mrs. Forester," Kay told her sincerely. "If it hadn't been for you giving me this room and helping in my support I wouldn't be able to attend school at all this year."

For an instant, but only for an instant, a strange look came into Mrs. Forester's eyes. "We're only too happy to be able to help you."

That evening after dinner Mrs. Forester came into the living room where Kay and Marilyn were sitting.

"We're having a meeting at my church this evening," she said. "Would you girls like to go with me?"

"What is it, Mother?" Marilyn asked. "We've got a little studying to do, but–."

"I don't think this will last very long," Mrs. Forester continued. "We have a woman from Minneapolis coming up to give us a book review on that new novel on the migration problem, *Between Two Trees*."

"I–I don't believe I would care to go," her daughter answered. "I know it will be good and all of that, but–."

Mrs. Forester bristled. "*But* it's in my church, so you don't care to go. Is that it?"

"It isn't that it's held in your church, Mother," Marilyn told her. "We're so busy that we don't have time for that sort of thing. Besides, it would be better if things like that were left to women's clubs and secular groups, and if the church would stick to the Gospel."

"Now you're being critical, my dear."

She went alone to the book review that evening. And when it was over, she approached Dr. Carpenter.

"I have a favor I would like to ask of you."

"Now what is that, Mrs. Forester?" he smiled without effort. "With what may I help you?"

"You know how concerned I've been about Marilyn," she said, "especially now that she's going to that fanatical school and is getting more wrapped up in that sort of thing all the time."

"I'm afraid it would do little good to try to talk to her."

"It wouldn't do any good for anyone to talk to her," Mrs. Forester agreed. "But I thought you might find something she could do here in the church, something that might help to wean her away from the people she's so concerned about now."

He pursed his lips.

"That would present some problems," he answered. "What do you have in mind?"

"She's been talking so much about working with young people. We have quite a group of high school youngsters. Perhaps you could ask Marilyn to help with them."

"As I say," the pastor replied reluctantly, "I'm afraid such an arrangement would present certain problems. You know, it wouldn't be a good influence for the harmony of our group to have Marilyn, or anyone else, bring in some of those teachings that might disturb our people."

Mrs. Forester's throat constricted, and her eyes filled with tears.

"Couldn't you use her in some capacity where she wouldn't have too much influence over the others?" she asked. "Perhaps you could have her help with the games or something like that. I know if we could get her under the influence of your ministry, she would adopt a reasonable attitude toward religion. That's what I want more than anything."

He stroked his chin thoughtfully. "She plays the piano nicely. Would she play for our square dancing?"

"I'm afraid she wouldn't do that. She's so straight-laced that she wouldn't even think of going to a dance, let alone playing for one. That's the sort of fanaticism that disturbs me."

"I wish there were some way I could help you," he said. "I know how concerned you are for her. If every mother were as interested in the welfare of her daughter, I'm sure this world would be a better place in which to live."

"Then you will help me?" Mrs. Forester pleaded. "I've tried my best to be sweet and considerate, the way you told me. But I can't carry on alone much longer. I've got to have help, Dr. Carpenter."

He smiled.

"Yes," he said, "I'll help you. I don't know just what I can do, nor what would be the best way to approach the matter, but I think I can do something. Marilyn is a good girl, Mrs. Forester, and a reasonable girl. She's blinded temporarily by these people who have such a narrow view of the Scriptures, and such outmoded ideas. But you don't need to worry. She'll come around."

Mrs. Forester beamed.

"How can I ever repay you?" she asked him.

CHAPTER 5

PLOTTING AGAIN

Roxie Orlis was voted into the Pep Club together with Susan and two other freshmen at the first meeting of that organization. "We made it!" Susan cried exultantly as soon as the meeting was over.

Roxie seemed to walk home on air.

"You don't know what this means to me, Danny," she told her older brother breathlessly. "There were only four freshman girls elected. And I was one of them!"

"It's all right to be popular," Danny said, "as long as we're popular in the right things."

She looked at him queerly.

That night the young people met at church, but Roxie did not go.

"They're having a meeting of the Pep Club tonight," she explained to Ron. "And I couldn't miss that. It's the first meeting they've had since I've been elected. What would the girls think of me if I didn't go?"

"I think they would understand," Ron answered.

"That doesn't mean I'm going to drop out of Young People's," Roxie told him firmly.

* * *

In a few days Dr. Carpenter made a visit to the Forester home.

"Mother isn't here," Marilyn said, ushering him into the living room. "I thought she would be back by now."

"Oh, that's all right!" the minister replied. "I'll just step in and wait." He followed her into the living room and sat down. "As a matter of fact, Marilyn, I came to see you as much as your mother."

"Me?"

"Should that be such a surprise?"

"Oh, no." Marilyn's voice trailed away.

"We have a fine Young People's work at our church," Dr. Carpenter said. "But we need some competent help to keep it moving forward. I've gone over our membership list and have talked with several, but I haven't been able to find exactly the right person.

Marilyn said nothing.

He leaned back in the chair and crossed his legs. "Do you think you could find the time to help us?"

She straightened suddenly.

The minister continued. "I know you've been attending another church, and that you're going to the Bible Institute which makes certain demands upon your time. But after all, you worshiped with us for years."

"I'd have to think about it, Dr. Carpenter," Marilyn told him.

When he was gone, she went into the kitchen where Kay was ironing a dress.

"I wouldn't do it at all if it weren't for Mother," Marilyn explained, "but there has been such a big difference in her the past few weeks. And she would be so pleased if I'd help Dr. Carpenter until he could find someone else."

"How could you hope to serve the Lord there? Dr. Carpenter says that he believes in salvation the same as we do, but he preaches that everyone is going to be saved if they do the best they can. And he says we don't have to believe Christ is God's only Son, but simply try to follow Him as our pattern because He was a good man, a great teacher."

"I'm going to pray about it," Marilyn assured her.

* * *

There was a hint of frost in the air, and Ron and Dick Masters intensified preparations for operating their trap line. They walked over it several times, noting the good places to make their sets. As they did so Ron talked with Dick about the Lord.

"I don't understand what you mean about this 'being saved' business," Dick told him. "It doesn't make sense to me."

"The Bible tells us that unless we're converted, unless we confess our sin and put our trust in the Lord Jesus to save us, we're lost."

"I live all right. Besides, I'm not going to die for a long time."

"Why don't you go to Sunday school with me," Ron asked him, "and to Young People's?"

"I'm too busy on Sunday mornings. We always sleep late or read the funny papers or go fishing in the summer. And sometimes Dad makes me mow the yard if I don't get it done Saturday afternoon."

"You should go with me a couple of times to see what it's like," Ron urged. "I know you'd like it."

"Maybe I will," Dick told him offhandedly, "when I don't have anything else to do." And then he changed the subject quickly.

That evening Roxie went to the Pep Club meeting again rather than Young People's. Danny went up into Ron's room and sat down beside the desk. His younger brother looked up and pushed aside his books.

"Hi," the younger boy said.

"Ron," Danny said, "I want to ask you a couple of things."

"Sure," his younger brother grinned. "What have I done now?"

"Not a thing," Danny said. "I've been concerned about Roxie, though. How are things with her?"

Ron's face grew serious. "What do you mean?"

Danny hesitated. "I suppose all this is silly, but I can't help worrying about her. How is she doing spiritually? Is she as interested in the things of the Lord as she should be?"

Ron ran his fingers through his curly hair and closed his book.

"I've been wanting to talk to you about her, Danny," he said, "but I've kept putting it off. She doesn't seem to be much different than she's always been. She reads her Bible every night, and is still interested in Sunday school and church, but she skips Young People's for Pep Club. Frankly, I've been worried about her too."

"In what way?"

"She seems to be so interested in pretty clothes and in being popular at school," her twin confided. "Maybe all girls are like that when they get into high school, but I don't like it."

"I guess I've been so busy that I haven't paid much attention to her," Danny answered, "but the last few days I've noticed a few things that I haven't liked too well. Just what has she been like?"

Briefly Ron told him all that had happened since they had come to Cedarton to attend high school.

"It isn't that she's doing anything bad, Danny," he hastened to add. "I might even be imagining a lot of it."

"I don't think so. I've noticed some of it myself, and Kay said yesterday that she thought she had seen a change coming over Roxie. Do you suppose it would do any good if Kay or I talked with her?"

"It certainly didn't do any good for me to talk to her," Ron told him. "Wow, did she get mad! She told me that she was living just as good a Christian life as I am, and that she wasn't going to have me preaching at her!"

"I want to pray about it," the older boy continued, "and talk to Kay again. Roxie's a pretty girl and has the sort of personality that all the kids like. She's going to make many friends. There will be a lot of pressure on her to take part in dances and go to shows and things like that. She's going to have a rough time to live a consistent Christian life."

"I don't know why it's going to be so much worse for her than it is for you and me," Ron retorted hotly.

* * *

Marilyn Forester had expected her mother to be pleased when she learned that Dr. Carpenter had been over and asked her to help with the Young People's work at First Church. However, she apparently was not too concerned.

"That is something that you will have to decide for yourself, Marilyn," she said. "I think you know how happy I would be if you could help Dr. Carpenter. After all, he has done so much for me. However, I wouldn't want it for that reason either."

"I'll pray about it, Mother," Marilyn assured her. Mrs. Forester put her arm about her daughter's shoulder affectionately.

"Thank you, darling," she said. Her voice choked. "Don't let what I want you to do influence you one way or the other. I want you to make the decision yourself."

The next day Marilyn talked to Dr. Nielsen about it.

"I know the Gospel isn't preached over there," she said, "but I do feel obligated because of Mother."

"You've asked me for my advice," he answered. "I wouldn't be honest with you if I didn't tell you what I believe. I'm afraid you would only be letting yourself in for trouble." He leaned forward earnestly. "If you go along with what Dr. Carpenter advocates it might hurt your testimony. If you stand up for what you believe and try to reach the young people who go there, I'm afraid you won't last very long."

"But Mother has been so sweet about it all," Marilyn countered. "And neither she nor Dr. Carpenter has tried to pressure me."

"The decision is one that you'll have to make, Marilyn," the Bible Institute president said gently.

"All I can do is to give you the benefit of my experience. I would advise against it, but you pray definitely for guidance, and wait upon the Lord until He gives you His answer."

CHAPTER 6

DRIFTING?

Marilyn and Kay prayed much about the work Dr. Carpenter had asked her to take; however, there was no answer. The more they prayed the more perplexed Marilyn became.

"I don't know what to do, Kay," she said when they got to their feet after a long session of prayer. I'm as undecided now as I was when Dr. Carpenter first talked to me about it."

Marilyn walked slowly over to the window where she stood looking out on the darkened street below.

"I've got to make up my mind one way or another right away. He called again this afternoon and I told him that I would give him a definite answer the day after tomorrow."

Mrs. Forester's attitude toward the young people from the Bible Institute seemed to change a great deal since school began. In the past few weeks she insisted that Marilyn invite some of her school friends.

"They're so clean and fresh and wholesome," she explained. "It's really a pleasure to have them around."

"I'm so glad you feel that way, Mother," Marilyn had beamed.

"Of course," Mrs. Forester's eyes narrowed slightly, "I would like them even better if they weren't so–so fanatical about their religion. That's one thing I like about the way Dr. Carpenter preaches. He's so practical and so soothing. There isn't any of that fear that's characteristic of so many other ministers. When you go home after listening to a message of his, you feel as though God is so close and so real, that you–you could love everybody."

"That's the way the Gospel should make us feel, Mother," Marilyn answered. "Of course, a minister isn't really worth his trust if he doesn't preach about the dangers of postponing a decision about the Lord Jesus. We've got to be warned about what will happen if we don't take Christ as our Savior."

Mrs. Forester drew herself up haughtily.

"I find myself very comforted listening to Dr. Carpenter."

She pouted for a while, but when Danny and Chuck came over an hour or so later to make some plans to give out tracts on Halloween night, she was as charming as ever. At the close of the evening, she came down to the basement with a plate full of sandwiches and some cold drinks.

"Your mother is a lovely person, Marilyn," Chuck said.

"She's been so good to me." And then the smile faded from her eyes. "If only we could get her to see that being good isn't enough. If only we could get her to see that she can't be saved by good works, attending church, and giving generously. If she could just understand that she's got to put her trust in the Lord Jesus, everything would be perfect."

"I got a letter from Tim today," Danny said after a time.

Marilyn's face lighted.

He unfolded the letter and began to read.

"You should be here for football, Danny," Tim had written. "I've learned more about blocking and ball-carrying in the past month than I ever thought anyone knew. And are we going to have a team next year! We've got the biggest Freshman squad that Crestwood ever had. And the whole Varsity line will be back again. I've been quarterbacking the Frosh since the second week of practice. Looks as though I'll get the starting nod next fall. If you were here everything would be wonderful. One of these days I'll drive home and let you see my car. It's a beauty."

"Boy, that guy's wrapped up in football, isn't he?" Chuck put in. "Does he do anything else?"

"He's a cool guy," Danny said defensively. "He

wouldn't have been able to go to school at all if he hadn't taken the football scholarship that was offered to him."

"Read the rest of his letter, please," Marilyn suggested.

Danny read on about the classes, and the way the people of the community treated the football players.

"We're really the kingpins around here," he wrote. "I've got a job in one of the stores, but the boss doesn't care too much whether I'm there or not. He told me that what he's interested in the most is a touchdown on Saturday afternoon. Of course, I've tried to keep my testimony by being on the job. I've been attending church too. The guy who told you that we couldn't be Christians and go to a school like Crestwood didn't know what he was talking about. We don't make such a fuss about it, but I think you could call Crestwood a Christian school. They have dances on the campus, and I guess a couple of the Frat houses have bars in the basements, but in general, the attitude of the school is pretty much Christian. You'd really like it here...."

There was more to the letter, but Danny didn't finish reading it.

Marilyn pursed her lips thoughtfully. "What do you think, Danny? What is Crestwood going to do to him?"

"I felt a little sick inside," Kay said, "when he wrote about dances on the campus and that sort of thing."

"But Tim didn't say he approved," Danny protested. "He just mentioned them."

"That's just the trouble. That sort of thing sneaks up on you. You're thrown in with people who dance and drink. At first it shocks you, but you see so much of it that it doesn't bother you after a while. Then you begin to think that it's all right for somebody else. When you get to that place, you're only about half a step from doing it yourself.

Chuck Martin agreed vigorously.

"I know how it is. I attended a school where that sort of thing went on. I got so calloused that I didn't think anything about smoking and drinking and dancing, or any of those things. I'm ashamed of it now, but I actually started to smoke last year. And when I first went up to Bible Camp last summer, I would sneak out two or three times a day to puff on a cigarette. It wasn't until I consecrated my life to the Lord Jesus that I began to see that I shouldn't smoke. And I had definite convictions about that sort of thing when I first went to college."

Danny went home that night greatly disturbed. He tried to write a letter to Tim, but the words wouldn't come. He was sitting there, chewing on his pen, when Roxie knocked on his door.

"Danny," she called, "are you awake?"

"Come on in."

She sat on the chair beside the door.

"I'm sorry I didn't go to Young People's the other night. I won't let the Pep Club interfere anymore."

"I'm glad to hear you say that, Roxie. There are a lot of pressures put on you at school. If you start letting those things interfere with your church and the activities of the church, they can really hurt your testimony."

"I don't know why you and Ron are always talking about me hurting my testimony," she said petulantly. "I'm as concerned about living for the Lord as you are in having me live for Him. I don't want to do anything to hinder my faith."

"Sometimes we do those things, and actually aren't aware of them until it's too late. That's the only thing that Ron and I have been worrying about. Someone else can see what's happening in our lives quicker than we see them."

"I don't know why it is that you're always thinking that I'm the one who's going to backslide. How about Ron? Aren't you worried about him?"

"We've all got to be concerned about ourselves all the time," Danny answered. "It's something that can happen to any of us, and when we least expect it. It isn't that we think you've done anything so terribly bad, Roxie. Or that we think you're more apt to drift away from the Lord than we are. But we both love you. We don't want to see you do things that would hurt our parents, and probably hurt you a great deal too."

"Well," she said curtly, getting to her feet, "you don't need to worry about me. I'm living just as consistently as Ron or any of the rest of those kids that are so careful about getting to Young People's every single time. I came in here tonight to tell you that I'm sorry for skipping Young People's. I didn't expect you to jump all over me."

"I'm sorry, Roxie," Danny started to apologize, but she turned and fled from the room, leaving him standing there.

He remained at the door for a long while, looking out into the dark, empty hall. Then he turned slowly and went back into his room.

The half-finished letter to Tim lay on the desk where he had left it when Roxie came in. He picked it up, read what he had written, then crumpled it into a ball and threw it into the wastebasket.

What could a guy do when people like Roxie and Tim began to drift from the Lord? How could you talk or write to them? He opened his Bible and read until long after the clock struck ten. Then he knelt beside the bed and began talking to God.

CHAPTER 7

MORE PRESSURE

Danny prayed a long time for Roxie. The clock struck midnight before he finally went to sleep. The next morning, he made it a point to meet Kay in the hall at school.

"Why don't we have lunch together? I've got to talk to you."

As they sat together in the cafeteria, he told her what had taken place the night before.

"What she says about backsliding is probably true in a way," Danny concluded. "It isn't as though she's drifted very far from the Lord. She's in Sunday school and church every week. And I know she's reading her Bible regularly and praying. But there's something about her attitude that bothers me. She's becoming so concerned about being popular at school, and not wanting to do anything that the kids might not like. I'm afraid if something isn't done that she's going to backslide, and badly."

"I think the Bible club did more to help me stay in tune with the Lord," Kay replied, "and made me want to live for Christ than any other single thing. Church and Young People's had their place, of course, but the Bible club was made up of kids our own age who were having the same problems we were having. Just knowing that we were all in the same boat together, and trying to live for the Lord, sort of gave me strength. And it kept us all eager to serve the Lord because we were always trying to get other kids to come."

"That might be the answer. Marilyn and Tim kept the Bible club going this summer, didn't they?"

Kay shook her head.

"They kept it going for a while, but Mr. Benton, the adult sponsor, moved away, and the group disbanded for the summer."

"Haven't they started again?"

Kay shook her head. "There was some talk of it at the first of the school term, but there didn't seem to be any real interest, so the matter was dropped."

Danny toyed with his glass of milk.

"Do you suppose we could get it in operation again?" he asked. "We're supposed to have a project of some sort as a part of our schoolwork."

"I've got a Sunday school class over at church, Danny, and most of the other kids are doing practical Christian work, but maybe someone could take on the Bible club."

"Why don't we talk with Dr. Nielsen about it right now?"

He was interested immediately.

"That is an oversight on our part," he said. "We've had so many things to take care of the past few weeks, with registration and all, that it didn't even occur to me that no one had set the high school Bible club into operation this year."

He frowned and reached in his desk for a sheaf of paper which he studied carefully.

"I think almost everybody is assigned now."

"Perhaps we could find somebody on the faculty who would sponsor the Bible club," Danny suggested. "Or someone in town."

"A Bible club would probably be as good training as our students could possibly get anywhere."

Danny and Kay got up to go.

"Why don't you pray about it?" Dr. Nielsen said. "I'll do the same. You can see me again in a day or two."

Outside the office Kay stopped.

"Danny," she said, "do you suppose the Lord is calling you to take the Bible club?"

"I couldn't handle a Bible club," he answered quickly. "I haven't had any experience with kids, nor Bible training either. I'd be lost."

"I know how you feel," Kay said. "It scares me to think of the responsibility of such a job. But if God is calling, He will give you the ability and wisdom you need."

"God would call a better person than me for that job," Danny said fervently. "I couldn't handle it."

That evening when Kay returned home from school Marilyn was up in her room changing clothes.

"And where are you going tonight? Is Chuck coming again?"

Marilyn shook her head, flushing a little.

"I've finally decided to take over that job at First Church."

"Are you sure it's the best thing, Marilyn?"

"I couldn't turn Mother down." Marilyn paused. "I don't know what I'll be doing yet, but Dr. Carpenter assured me that I would have absolute freedom. Perhaps I can be a Christian testimony there."

She was leaving the house when Chuck Martin came up on the porch.

"How did you know that I was going to come and ask you to go to the concert with me, Marilyn?" he asked gaily. "I didn't even know it myself until half an hour ago."

"For your information, Mr. Martin," Marilyn bantered, "I'm going to First Church to help with the Young People's."

"So, Daniel's going into the lions' den, eh? Guess I'll have to go along and see what happens."

They walked off the porch together.

"But you can't go with me, Chuck. You haven't been invited."

"Oh, yes, I have!" he told her. "I invited myself. Just a little while ago."

"Now what do you mean by that?"

"I called Dr. Carpenter and told him that I knew a charming young man who would be delighted to help you with your share of the program. He was overjoyed."

"You didn't!"

"Didn't I, though? I assured him that I had two years of college. That I am a young man with good habits and a good name. And that I had a personal interest in seeing that Miss Marilyn Forester succeeds."

"You wouldn't dare!" she exclaimed horrified.

"To tell you the truth," Chuck said seriously, "Dr. Nielsen asked me to help you a few times. I've had a little experience with Young People's work, and he thought it might be better if two of us were there. He called Dr. Carpenter and made the arrangements."

Marilyn sighed deeply.

"I'm glad to have you along," she confessed. "To be honest with you, Chuck, I'm scared to death."

At school, the Freshman class held an election on the first Tuesday in November, and Roxie was elected secretary. But this time she took it in stride.

"I wish they would have elected Ron," Roxie told Susan when the two of them walked home together after the class meeting. "He doesn't get into anything."

"I wouldn't worry about him if I were you. He would have gotten into everything if he had wanted to. Coach Hanson pleaded with him to go out for football, but no, he had to run his old trap line."

Roxie said something to Ron about it when she got home.

"Don't let that bother you. Dick and I are having a terrific time."

* * *

The first responsibility of the Freshman class officers was to plan a party. They held a meeting Thursday night after school in the home room of the class sponsor. As soon as Roxie came home, Ron knew there was something wrong.

"What's the matter?" Ron asked. "You act as though you'd just swallowed a worm."

"Don't be so funny, Ron," she retorted. "You try to make a joke out of everything."

She sat down at the desk she and Karen shared in their room. Ron pulled up a chair and sat down across from her.

"I didn't mean to upset you," he told her, apologizing. "What's the trouble?"

For almost a minute Roxie sat there, working her hands intently. "It's the class party," she said at last. "I tried to fight against it. But the other kids wouldn't even listen to me."

"Suppose you start at the beginning."

"Well! Our class sponsor said that we should have a party before long. They had wanted to have a Halloween party, but we didn't have our election of officers soon enough, so we thought we'd have an early Thanksgiving party."

"I don't see anything so wrong about that."

Roxie got up and walked across the room.

"But this isn't just an ordinary party," she said. "They're going to have a theater party. They said there was a good show in town that night and everybody would want to see it. So they voted to get together as a class and go to the show. They called the theater and got special prices and everything."

Ron was silent.

"It wasn't my fault, Ron," she protested almost tearfully. "I suppose you and Danny will say that it was, but it wasn't. I did everything I could to keep them from having a theater party."

"Did you tell them why you didn't want it?" Ron asked her pointedly.

For an instant Roxie's eyes flashed.

"What difference does it make?" she demanded. "They outvoted me. And the last thing the sponsor said was that we would all have to get behind it, if we wanted it to be a success. She said every officer had to be there."

"That's tough." Ron eyed her critically. "What do you plan to do?"

She looked up, appealingly.

"What can I do?" she wailed. "I'm one of the officers and I'm expected to be there. What can I do?"

CHAPTER 8

A WORTHWHILE TRY

There were twenty or thirty young people at the First Church when Marilyn Forester and Chuck Martin arrived to help with the meeting. Dr. Carpenter came forward to greet them.

"I'm so happy to have you young people with us," he said, smiling widely. "It's so difficult to find anyone who's really concerned about church work anymore."

He guided them into a little room off the main basement.

"Here is a lesson book our denomination puts out," Dr. Carpenter said. "If you wish to follow it, I'm sure you would have a fine meeting."

"I think Marilyn is already prepared, Dr. Carpenter," Chuck answered.

"That's fine." His eyes squinted speculatively. "You aren't going to be fanatical about it are you, Marilyn?"

"We're just going to bring the Gospel," Chuck broke in. "You wouldn't call that fanatical, would you?"

"Oh, no!" the minister answered quickly. "No. Certainly not. I preach the Gospel myself."

Chuck called the meeting to order and led the kids in a few songs. They didn't know any of the choruses, but he taught them two or three, and they sang lustily. The minister sat in the back of the room for a few minutes, then got up and left. When the singing was over Marilyn started the lesson.

She began with John 3:1, and went slowly, sentence by sentence, explaining what Christ meant. At first the young people sat there, listening silently. Then hands began to go up.

"What does that mean about being 'born again'?" a tall, slender sophomore asked. "I never heard anything like that before."

Patiently Marilyn and Chuck explained the way of salvation. A flood of questions followed. Some of the questions were so simple that a child should have been able to answer them. Others were so profound that Chuck and Marilyn looked at one another helplessly.

"I'll have to talk to one of the instructors out at school about this," Marilyn said in answer to one question. "Be sure and remind me to give you his answer at the next meeting."

It was 9 o'clock and the interest showed no sign of lagging when Dr. Carpenter came back and sat down.

When the service was over the minister approached Marilyn and Chuck and thanked them.

"I've never seen such interest in our young people," he said. "I only wish I could have been here for the entire meeting."

When the two young people returned to Marilyn's home, Mrs. Forester met them at the door.

"Come in, children," she beamed. "I just had a telephone call from Dr. Carpenter. He told me that the meeting went over splendidly tonight. Splendidly."

She ushered them into the kitchen where she had prepared lunch and sat down with them, asking the blessing herself. Marilyn looked up at her in surprise. It was the first time that had happened.

* * *

Danny and Kay prayed about the Bible club as Dr. Nielsen had suggested, and talked with their pastor and two or three others in the church they thought might be interested. The answer was always the same. Everyone was interested, but no one seemed to have the time to do anything about it.

"Now I know what it is that makes a pastor's life so hard," Danny Orlis said wearily as they walked back to the Forester house. "We've talked to people who aren't as busy as we are, but they don't have any time to work with the Bible club."

"We haven't talked to anyone who would be willing to help with it," she said. "That's certain."

The next morning, they went to see the President of the Bible Institute.

"Do you still have the same burden for this Bible club that you did before?" he asked.

They both nodded.

"Even more so, if possible," the Orlis boy said with determination. "We've got to get that Bible club started."

"Did it ever occur to you, Danny," the President went on in the same kindly tone, "that perhaps the Lord is talking to you in this matter? He's put the burden upon your heart. You haven't been able to find anyone else to do it. Perhaps that's God's way. Perhaps He wants you and Kay to take over this Bible club."

"But we haven't had any training," Danny replied.

"We were both in a Bible club," Kay said, "and I'm sure that Dr. Nielsen would help us where he could."

The President picked up his pencil and fingered it thoughtfully.

"God wants us to be prepared," he told them. "That's why we have Bible institutes and colleges.

But He also wants consecration, willing hearts. He wants us to be ready to do the things He calls us to do. I'm convinced in my own mind, that if the two of you honestly feel the burden of this thing, it must be God's will that you do it." He smiled warmly. "If that's the case you can look to Him for all the help and guidance you'll need," he went on. "Personally, I think it is a wonderful opportunity to serve the Lord."

"Well," Danny said reluctantly, "I'm willing to try it. But God is certainly going to have to do the guiding. I get petrified every time I think of taking on something like this."

"I'm so excited," Kay said when they were outside of Dr. Nielsen's office. "I just know that we can take over the Bible club and reach a lot of those high school kids. We got acquainted with so many when we were here in school. That might help us to get them out."

"I hope you're right," Danny said dubiously.

* * *

Ron was as happy and excited as Kay when Danny told him what they planned to do.

"I'm going to get hold of some of those guys in our class," he exclaimed. "They should be interested in the Bible club."

"That's just the kind of help we're going to need," Danny said. "You and Kirk and Karen and Roxie can do a lot to get a good turnout for us."

"When are you going to have the first meeting?" his younger brother wanted to know. "Tomorrow night?"

"Not so fast. I have to get the lesson prepared. We have to find a place to hold the meeting and everything."

"I'm going to start talking it up, anyway," Ron continued. "Dick Masters is the first one I'm going to work on. Maybe we can get him out to the Bible club."

Roxie acted as though she were glad that the Bible club was being reorganized, but Danny wondered, as he talked with her, just how deep her interest was.

"I think some of the kids would really like it," she said.

"Do you suppose that you could interest some of your friends?"

A strange look flashed across Roxie's face. "I don't know," she told him. "Some of them go to other churches, and some don't go to any. I don't know how they'd take it if I talked to them."

"We aren't going to try to get them away from their home churches, Roxie. It'll be good Christian fellowship for those who know Christ as their Savior, and those who don't go to church at all are the ones that we need to reach. Would you talk to some of them for us?"

"I–I'll see what they have to say."

The following evening was the night of the Freshman class party. Ron had intended to talk with Danny about it. In fact, at one time he was about to mention it, but he didn't.

"I suppose you're going to run and tell Danny that I'm going to the show tonight, Ron," Roxie said in an angry whisper after supper was over and they were upstairs alone.

"I haven't said anything to him," Ron answered. "But I sure wish you weren't going."

She laid her hand on his arm.

"Don't you understand, Ron? Honestly!"

"I sure wish you wouldn't," was all that Ron could say.

She turned and stomped into the bedroom and slammed the door.

Later Susan stopped by for her.

Roxie felt a little sick to think she was actually on her way to the theater. She had often heard her mother and dad talk against them, explaining why it was better for a Christian to stay away from shows. But this was different, she told herself doggedly. She wouldn't enjoy a minute of it. She was only going because she had to.

"This is going to be a swell show," Susan said as they approached the gym where everyone was to meet. "I saw a preview of it last night. Oh, it's exciting! There's a place where this guy gets drunk, see? And kills his wife, and–."

Roxie shuddered.

The other girls came crowding up to Roxie and Susan as they entered the gym.

"Oh, you've got a new dress on, Susan!" one of them exclaimed. "It's beautiful!"

"Lane Department Store, $59.95," Susan sang out.

Roxie winced. Her entire wardrobe hadn't cost that much. Mother had bought material and had sewed early and late to make dresses for her to wear to school.

"I don't really like this dress," Susan said when the others had gone. "I don't think I'll wear it anymore."

"Not wear it?"

"Oh, I've got lots of dresses that I've worn only two or three times!" she answered.

"But what do your parents think?" Roxie asked, shocked.

"Oh, Dad growls around a little, but I just go down to the store and charge them! He never makes me take them back."

They went to the theater then. Roxie hung back, reluctantly, until all the others were in.

"Come on, Roxie," Susan said. "It will start in a few minutes."

"I–I–," she said.

"Here," Susan said, "give me your money. I'll buy the tickets."

Numbly Roxie handed her friend the money and Susan bought the tickets. They went in and sat down. Before long, the previews came on.

Roxie was scarcely watching. Questions started to hammer through her mind. "What if Jesus should return tonight and find me here?" she kept asking herself repeatedly.

CHAPTER 9

SHE COULDN'T STAY

At the theater, the preview of the pictures was being shown. Roxie's eyes filled with tears. Her mind was reeling. She knew she couldn't stay in the theater another moment. She got up and started to push past Susan.

"Where are you going?" her friend whispered. "The feature is going to start in a couple of minutes." Roxie did not answer her. She reached the aisle and fled.

People in the lobby turned to stare at her as she went running past, the tears streaming down her face.

She reached home just as Danny was leaving to see Kay and work out plans for the first meeting of the Bible club.

"Is the party already over?" he asked. But she went by without speaking.

Once past him she stopped hesitantly and turned as though to face him.

"I don't care about their old party," she blurted. And before he had time to ask her more, she turned and fled into the house.

Roxie Orlis went into the room she shared with Karen, thankful that the other girl was gone, and closed the door. For a long while she stood there, motionless in the darkness. Then, switching on the light, she picked up her Bible and tried to read.

But the words blurred before her eyes. She had known she shouldn't go to the theater. Even while they were planning it, she had known. She had known when she got dressed earlier that evening, and when she walked down to the gym with Susan. But she had gone. And now she was miserable.

She dropped in agony beside her bed and tried to pray, but somehow the thoughts kept crowding in.

She could have told the other girls that she couldn't go to the party if she had decided before getting inside the theater. She wouldn't have had to give them a reason. They'd have thought she had to study, or that Danny had heard where they were going and was furious.

But now they knew. Everyone in school would know in the morning. She'd be the laughing stock of the Freshman class.

"But what difference did that make?" she asked herself. Like Ron said, why should she care if people knew that she loved the Lord Jesus and wanted to follow Him? Why should it matter to anyone whether she thought it was right to go to a movie or not?

There on her knees she decided exactly what she was going to say to Susan and the others in the morning. She knew they would crowd about her when she came to school, eager to find out why. She was going to tell them about Christ, and what it meant to follow Him. She was going to explain the way of salvation if they'd listen.

Susan went to church once in a while, to the same church Mrs. Forester attended. But she didn't know what it meant to be saved. Roxie could tell that by the things she said about Ron and Danny and their ideas of separation. Roxie would go through the whole plan of salvation with her. Perhaps she could get her to come to Bible club. She might even be able to lead Susan to Christ.

Finally, after what seemed to be an hour or two, but was actually much less, she got to her feet and changed into her pajamas. When Karen came in a short time later Roxie kept her eyes tightly closed. She just couldn't talk to anyone right then.

The next morning when Roxie went down to breakfast Danny looked at her strangely.

"Are you sure you feel all right, Roxie?"

"Of course." She avoided his eyes.

Ron looked as though he were going to blurt out the truth about the party, but she cast a warning glance at him, and he said nothing.

As she suspected, Susan was waiting for her around the corner when she went to school.

"What was the matter with you last night that you left the theater so quickly?" the other girl asked anxiously.

Roxie Orlis felt the color come up into her cheeks. Once or twice, she tried to speak, but her tongue was like cotton and her heart began to pound in her throat.

"I–I–."

"Were you ill?" Susan repeated.

"I–I had a terrible headache," Roxie said reluctantly. The lie lingered like acid on her tongue, burning relentlessly. Why was she so ashamed of the Lord? Why didn't she tell Susan the real reason why she left the theater? She had planned to do it, but again she had failed.

"The other girls said it was because you were so religious that you wouldn't go to a movie. But I told them they didn't know what they were talking about."

Roxie's face went scarlet. She tried to tell Susan. She tried to find the words to give her testimony. But her friend was rattling on, telling her about the show she had missed. When Roxie finally went to her first class of the morning, she had the headache she had told Susan she had had the night before.

* * *

Mrs. Meyer insisted that Danny and Kay hold the first meeting of the Bible club at their home.

"I'll fix some cold drinks and cookies," she told the older Orlis boy, "and we'll have a little party afterward. Maybe it will help to get the group off to a good start."

Ron and Kirk talked with many of the kids at school, and Karen invited some of her friends. Roxie tried, timidly, to get Susan to come, but the latter dismissed the idea easily. And, despite all the efforts that had been made to get a good turnout, the group that gathered at the Meyer home was small and unenthusiastic.

"I told you I couldn't do it," Danny said miserably to Kay when the last of the high school kids had gone, and the two of them were in the kitchen helping Mrs. Meyer with the dishes. "I knew I couldn't manage **it.**"

"But we can't say the meeting tonight wasn't a success," Kay replied, "just because the group was small. We knew before we started that it wasn't going to be easy."

She smiled encouragingly.

"I guess you're right at that," Danny agreed.

Upstairs Roxie switched out the light and got ready for bed. A cold, dull ache had taken hold of her heart. She was miserable.

The following morning on the way to school, Kay and Marilyn waited for Danny at the street corner across from the post office.

"I got a letter from Tim," Marilyn said, smiling. "He's going to be home Wednesday."

"Boy, that's swell!" Danny answered.

"He asked me to tell you and Kay not to plan anything while he's home. He said the four of us are really going to do the town."

"How is he coming?" Kay asked. "By train?"

"Oh, no!" Marilyn replied quickly, and with a trace of pride in her voice. "He's going to drive his new car. You remember, they gave him one for going down there to play football."

"Do you suppose he'll be here in time for the Union Thanksgiving Service Wednesday evening?" Danny asked. "It would be fun if we could all go together, wouldn't it?"

Mr. and Mrs. Forester invited Danny to have dinner with them on Wednesday evening.

"I know you'll want to be with the twins and Mr. and Mrs. Meyer tomorrow," Mrs. Forester said when she called him.

* * *

"Good evening, Danny," Harold Forester said warmly when the young woodsman appeared. "We're glad to have you. Have you seen Tim?"

Danny shook his head. "He isn't home yet, is he?"

"I saw him early this afternoon," Harold Forester said. "I invited him for dinner tonight too."

Danny walked in and stood for a moment before the fireplace.

"I thought he would look me up when he got here."

"Perhaps his mother didn't want him to leave so soon after getting home," Marilyn said defensively. "She's out there all alone now and hasn't seen him since school started."

Mrs. Forester came bustling in from the kitchen. "Is everybody here?"

"Tim Barton hasn't come yet, Mother," Mr. Forester told her.

She wrinkled her nose distastefully.

"I might have known he would be the one to keep us waiting," she said petulantly. "Why did you invite him, Harold? He scarcely fits in; with the sort of father he has and everything."

Marilyn winced at the fire in her mother's voice.

"We can wait until seven," Mr. Forester said, looking at his watch. "That will still give us an hour to eat and get down to the church in time for the service."

"It's going to seem so good for all of us to go to church together," Mrs. Forester said. "It will seem almost like it did years ago when we all attended First Church together."

Seven o'clock came, and 7:10, but still Tim did not arrive.

"I don't see how we can possibly wait any longer," Mrs. Forester wailed. "Everything is almost ruined as it is."

"Why don't you call his place, Danny?" Mr. Forester suggested.

The Orlis boy went to the phone and dialed the number. Mrs. Barton answered. She sounded as though she had been crying.

In a few moments he turned to the others, after setting the receiver back in its cradle. "I guess we might just as well go ahead and eat," he said.

"Isn't Tim coming?" Marilyn asked. There was concern in her voice. "Are you sure you saw him, Daddy? Maybe he hasn't come home yet."

Danny hesitated an instant.

"He got home all right," he said. "His mother told me that he came bustling into the house about half an hour ago. Another guy and two girls were in the car. He changed clothes in a hurry and drove away. He didn't say where he was going, nor when he would be back."

CHAPTER 10

WHAT A CHANGE!

Thanksgiving morning was cold and blustery. The clouds were hanging low over the little Northern Minnesota community, and there was a hint of snow in the air. At the filling station up the street from the Meyer home, car owners were checking the antifreeze in their radiators.

"What's the matter with you, Roxie?" Ron asked, coming into the living room where his twin sister was sitting alone. "You act as though you've lost your last friend."

She looked up slowly.

"I've been thinking about our parents and wondering what they're doing," she said. There was a tear in her voice. "This is the first time we've been away from them for Thanksgiving, Ron, since we went up there to live."

"But it won't be long until we'll be home for

Christmas," he answered. "It would cost too much for you and me and Danny to go home. And besides, there isn't enough time off from school for us to go that far."

"I can't help feeling a little lonesome," she said. "Did you ask Danny if we got a letter this morning?"

The older Orlis boy came into the room just then. "I'm going to the post office right now. Want to go along, Ron?"

"I promised Dick I'd look after the trap line this morning. And I'm going to have to hurry, or I won't get back in time for the service."

Danny got into his coat and went out into the crisp morning air. There had been little snow yet, but the weather reports were promising it, and it felt as though it wouldn't be long in coming. The Orlis boy pulled his coat collar tighter about his neck and quickened his pace. He didn't even notice the car come up alongside him and stop until a horn blasted raucously.

"Hi, Danny!" Tim Barton called out, leaning over and opening the door of the bright yellow convertible. "Long time no see. Where are you going?"

"Tim!" Danny exclaimed. "When did you get in? How are things at Crestwood?"

"Never better," Tim smiled broadly. "How do you like her? She'll do 110 on the straight-away."

Danny looked the car over appraisingly. It was

one of the smaller makes, but it had a radio, heater, dual horns, and plenty of chrome.

"Boy, this is some car!" Danny whistled.

"You should see the rig that All-State back from Texas got for enrolling at Crestwood," Tim said depreciatingly. "It makes this one look like a toy."

Danny got in beside him and Tim reached across his lap to close the door.

"I should have held out a little longer. I could have done better too."

Danny said nothing. He could have had a car like this too, and just for playing football. For a moment a wave of jealousy surged through him.

"We missed you over at the Foresters last night," he said then.

"I planned on getting over there. But I met Dennis Melton and a couple of girls up town. They insisted that I take them for a ride. We went out and had dinner together and then fooled around for a while. To tell you the truth, Danny, I forgot all about going to the Foresters."

There was a short silence.

"Just imagine Dennis Melton wanting to run around with me," Tim added, more to himself than to his companion. "He wouldn't even speak to me when we were going to high school. And I guess I can't blame him for that. His dad's the town's banker, and mine's the town's drunk."

Danny twisted in the seat to look at Tim. His

friend was older and heavier, and there was an air of arrogance about him; a strange, superior attitude that had never been there before.

"Is Crestwood all you had hoped it would be?" Danny asked him.

"You've never been in such a place, Danny. The football players are really the big wheels. They get nominated for the best fraternities and invited to the best parties. I don't know what they do at other colleges, but at Crestwood you hardly have to study at all if you play football. There's always somebody who'll help you do a paper if you get stuck on it. And the teachers almost always offer to give the football players a second exam if you have trouble on the first one." He turned out onto the highway and stepped down on the accelerator. The powerful motor leaped to life.

"Of course, I'm studying, Danny," he added quickly. "I really want to get an education."

"How are things spiritually, Tim? Do you still find time for the things of the Lord?"

The question was innocent enough, but it drove its barbs deeply into Tim Barton. His face flushed.

"I think I'm closer to Christ now, Danny, than when I was here in Cedarton going to school," he said. "I've been teaching a Sunday school class in a swell little church and have even gotten a couple of guys to go with me. The idea that you can't be a good Christian and go to Crestwood is a lot of baloney."

"I don't think anybody says that you can't be a good Christian and go to Crestwood," Danny corrected. "Those I've talked with simply have said that it was more difficult, and that a good many find the general atmosphere of such schools weakening to their faith."

"Well, it hasn't weakened mine," Tim retorted. "By the way, where were you headed? To the post office?"

Danny nodded.

"What are you and Marilyn and Kay going to do tonight, Danny?" Tim asked when Danny rejoined him after picking up the mail. "I'd like to make up for that deal last night." We could go out to dinner to the Royal Steak House. We were there last night. It's a wonderful place to eat."

Danny grinned. "You're not talking to me, fella," he said. "I'm just a poor Bible school student. I don't have the money to eat in a place like that."

"I invited you, didn't I?" Tim rejoined. He reached in his pocket and pulled out a small pack of bills. "I guess there should be enough here for us to eat on."

"What did you do, rob a bank?"

"I told you that they take care of their football players at Crestwood."

"Now, don't tell me that you got all that for playing football."

"As a matter of fact," Tim said, putting the money away, "I got this on the side. One of the alumni came down to the last Freshman game. He won quite a lot of money on the game, so he gave me a hundred of it. I made the winning touchdown."

Danny stared at him. "Do you mean that you took money like that?"

"And why not? There weren't any strings attached. They just came up and handed it to me. I'd be a sucker not to take it."

Danny stared at him. "Do you mean that you took money like that?" he repeated.

"I think we'd better go back toward Meyers'," he said after a moment or two. "Ron and Roxie are going to be wondering about this letter."

"Why don't you come out to the house with me for a while, Danny?" Tim urged. "I'd like to show you some of our football pictures. Boy, everything would be perfect, if you were just at Crestwood too."

He pulled over to the curb and stopped. "You could transfer, you know, Danny," he said. "You might lose a few credits, but I know they'd be glad to take you. If we had a scrapbook of your newspaper clippings, it would be a cinch to *get* you squared away with a car and everything. There are a lot of guys down there who are willing to go all out to help a football player."

"No!" Danny told him firmly. "I'm perfectly satisfied with where I am. I'm convinced that it was God's will for me to go to the Bible Institute for at least a couple of years before I think about getting an education anywhere else."

"You'll come out to the house with me, won't you?" Tim asked.

"I won't be able to stay long."

"That won't make any difference," Tim said. "You can help me a lot if you're there for a little while. I don't figure on staying any longer than I have to."

Danny looked at him. "What do you mean?"

"Oh, it's Mom! I don't know what's gotten into her. She's been pouring it onto me ever since I got home. I sleep too late. I don't stay home enough. I don't talk to her. I don't know what's wrong."

The Orlis boy was silent. He was thinking of his own mother, how anxious she was to see him after he had been away from home for a few months, how she asked a thousand questions. But then, he asked questions too.

"I thought your mother was a Christian now, Tim," Danny said.

"It isn't that," Tim said, stopping with a screech of the brakes in the driveway. "The only thing I can think of is that she's jealous because I've got a little money and a car. I don't know why she should be. She wanted me to go to Crestwood in the first place."

Danny started to get out, but Tim remained behind the wheel.

"She's always howling about how little dough she's got to live on," he said, "and how she has to scrimp and save and wear last year's dresses. Well, it isn't my fault. I've got all I can do to take care of myself at Crestwood. Now that the football season's over there won't be any extra money coming in, and it costs like everything to keep a car going."

Danny took a deep breath.

"Now that I'm living in a fraternity it seems that I'm always broke and borrowing from one of the frat brothers," Tim concluded.

"Your mother has had a rough time, Tim," Danny said. "She was sick for a while last month and wasn't able to work."

"It isn't that I'd mind helping her if I could," Tim retorted. "It's that yowling and nagging at me all the time. I can't stand it. If this keeps up, I don't think I'll even come home for Christmas."

CHAPTER 11

CHRISTMAS EVE AT THE ANGLE

Tim Barton had stayed in Cedarton as long as he could and headed back to college the Sunday morning following Thanksgiving. He was just leaving town when Danny and Kay started for Sunday school and stopped to give them a ride. "I'd like to stay for services," he said casually, "but the coach says we have to be in early. We really have to toe the line."

Danny looked up at him. "We'll be praying for you anyway, Tim."

Danny and Kay stood on the curb until the sleek, yellow convertible careened around the corner, screeched to a stop at the highway, and turned south.

"I'm really concerned about him, Danny," Kaye said at last. "Did you ever see such a change come over a person in so short a time?"

"I was thinking the same thing," the Orlis boy said. "He doesn't seem like the Tim Barton we knew at all."

"It's so easy for a Christian to backslide," Kay said slowly, "and so awfully hard to get back into the right relationship with the Lord.

* * *

Ronald Orlis and his partner began to work their traps every day, as the winter wore on.

"We've been making some good catches, Roxie," he said exuberantly to his sister one evening toward the middle of the week. "I've got most of my Christmas shopping already done."

The smile faded from her eyes and the corners of her mouth drooped slightly. "It doesn't look as though I'll be able to do any Christmas shopping this year, or even give the gift to missions that I've been planning on."

"Didn't Mother write last week and tell us that she was going to send us some money soon to buy a few gifts for Christmas?" Ron asked her.

Roxie nodded, swallowing hard. "But I won't be able to use the money for that."

Ron sat quietly without speaking.

"You know that Thanksgiving party at school last week?" Roxie asked at last. "Well, I went downtown with a couple of girls. They went into the dress shop and picked out dresses and charged them. And–and the man let me charge one too."

Ron stiffened and pushed aside his book. "Do you mean to tell me that you went to a store and charged a new dress?"

Roxie nodded miserably.

"And so you're going to use your Christmas money to pay for the new dress? Is that it?"

Roxie blinked hard as tears welled up in her eyes and sneaked, unnoticed, from beneath her eyelids.

"I had to have a dress for the party, Ron," she explained lamely, "and it just fit me."

"Now if it were some new traps I could understand it," he said, "but a dress! You've got a whole closet full of them!"

"I haven't been able to sleep, or even think about anything else since I did it," she blurted defensively. "I see now how wrong it was. But it's too late. I won't be able to buy Christmas gifts or anything."

"You don't need to try to talk me into putting your name on my packages," he told her indifferently. "When the rest of us are giving packages, you can go in and put on your new dress."

Roxie burst into tears and fled from the room.

Ron had thought that he didn't care, but all through the evening he found himself thinking about it. And before going to bed he went into Danny's room and told him what Roxie had done.

"I'm not at all surprised," Danny answered.

"Roxie's been so concerned about herself and being popular in school that she doesn't think about anyone except herself."

"What can we do about it?"

Danny shook his head. "It looks to me," he answered, "as though Roxie is going to have to get this thing straightened out herself."

"She's been bawling all day."

"You and I have our own gifts to the Lord's work that we want to make," Danny said, "and some Christmas presents to buy. Roxie had the same choice, but she made the wrong one. It'll be hard, but it's up to her to take care of it now."

* * *

There was a splendid turnout at Bible club the following evening. Several new boys and girls were there. And at the close of the service one boy talked with Danny about his soul.

"Wasn't that wonderful, Ron?" Roxie asked as the two of them walked home together through the snow. "To think that Danny was the one who was speaking when Louis came under conviction. It makes me feel that we should try to get all the boys and girls we know to come to Bible club."

Ron grinned at her.

"I'm going to talk to some of the girls the first thing

in the morning," she said with more determination than she had shown in several weeks.

"You sound more like the old Roxie tonight than any time since you've come to Cedarton to go to school."

"I don't feel like the old Roxie. I feel terrible. Nothing's right anymore. Everything seems to go wrong."

He started to tell her that he would help her pay for her dress. After all he did have a little extra money from his trapping. But he stopped suddenly. What was it Danny had said about making Roxie work things out for herself?

That evening Ron spent a long while on his knees, praying for the Bible club, for Danny, and for Roxie, who felt that she had just about ruined any enjoyment she would get from Christmas.

That evening after supper Roxie sought out Danny and told him, tearfully, about the dress. She started at the beginning, how she had charged the dress thoughtlessly, and now was going to have to take the money she was getting from home to pay for it.

"I'm going to have to spend all the money Mother's sending to pay for the dress. I'm not going to have anything to give to my special missionary offering at church or buy Christmas gifts or anything."

Danny nodded.

"Do you remember when you got that skirt and sweater at the beginning of the school year?" he asked her. "You know, it took money that I needed desperately for my schooling to pay for them."

"I–I know," she said softly. "I felt awful about it afterward."

"I wouldn't have done it, Roxie," he continued, "except that I thought it might help to teach you a lesson. We've got to make sacrifices. We can't have everything we want."

She swallowed hard. "I felt terrible about the skirt and sweater after I found out how you had sacrificed in order to get them for me. But I just didn't think about it when I wanted to buy the dress. The other girls were charging their dresses, and the man at the store said he'd charge one for me too, if I would promise to pay it when I got the money from home."

"What do you suppose would happen, Roxie," he asked her, "if something should come up at home so you couldn't get any money? How would you pay for the dress then?"

Her hand flew to her mouth. "I've never thought of that!"

There was a short silence.

"And what do you want me to do?"

"I don't know," Roxie blurted. "I don't know what anybody can do. But this is going to be the worst Christmas I've ever had!"

She was biting her lower lip to keep from crying.

Danny smiled for an instant.

"I'm not sure," he began, "but I think there is something you can do."

She looked up at him, her eyes brightening.

"It isn't going to be easy," he told her. "In fact, it might be very hard. You'll have to deny yourself some things you enjoy doing, and take some of the time that you would use for studying or running with the kids."

"I'll do anything," she answered him. "If I can just get that dress paid for and have enough money to give my gift to the Lord and buy a few presents for Christmas. I don't care if I'm not able to buy expensive gifts, but I want to have something to give at Christmas."

"Why don't you go down to the dress shop where you bought your dress," Danny suggested, "and see if they can use an extra girl between now and Christmas? Most of the stores need extra help right now."

"Oh, do you think I could get a job?" she cried.

"It might be hard work," Danny told her. "You'd probably be put to wrapping packages, or stocking shelves, or maybe even sweeping the floor."

"I don't care about that," she said. "I'll do anything, if I can just get this mess straightened out."

"I'm glad to hear you say that, Roxie."

"I've been praying and praying that God would help me."

"I think God has helped you to find an answer, Roxie. But you've got to be careful that you don't get into a mess like this again. Most of our troubles are of our own making, you know."

"Oh, you don't have to worry about me!" she said confidently. A little too confidently, Danny thought. "This will never happen again."

* * *

Even though there were two weeks' vacation from school, the days passed swiftly at Angle Inlet, and almost before they realized it, Christmas Eve was upon them.

Christmas Eve was bitter and cold. It had snowed the night before, and the wind had howled across Angle Bay to snatch up the newly fallen snow and hurl it against brush and trees and isolated buildings in great, soft piles. But, toward evening, the bleak winter sun shouldered aside the clouds and sent its pale, "warmthless" beams to play deceitfully on the frozen wastes. The wind ceased its blowing as darkness came, and the great, solemn hush of the northland locked its arms about the lake and muskeg once more. Even the snowbirds and ever-present sparrows seemed to fly on tiptoe lest they mar the sacred quiet of the evening.

But the silence of the evening had failed to penetrate the Orlis cabin. Logs, crackling merrily in the fireplace, sent a warm glow through the living room.

Kay sat at the old-fashioned organ, and Danny,

hovering over her, lifted his voice above the others as they sang Christmas carols.

Finally, Mrs. Orlis sighed. "I'd like to go on," she said, laughing a little. "I love those old songs. But honestly, we've sung so much that I don't think I can manage another note."

Kay turned around on the organ stool. "I'm about winded too," she said. "That pumping is hard work."

"What about the packages?"

"Why don't we go in by the fireplace, and have Danny read the Christmas story?" Carl Orlis suggested. "Somehow Christmas isn't complete without hearing Luke's account of it."

Danny Orlis took the Bible from the corner of the organ where he had laid it. He knew he would be asked to read some time before they opened their gifts. Ever since he had been old enough to master the difficult words, he had been reading the account of Christ's birth. And before that, his dad had read it.

Now he opened the Bible and began to read those old familiar words that he almost knew by heart.

"And it came to pass in those days," he read, "that there went out a decree from Caesar Augustus, that all the world should be taxed–."

As he read, they all listened intently. A faint smile played at the corners of Roxie's mouth. And silently she reached out her hand and took Kay's fingers, squeezing them affectionately.

"That's the most beautiful story in all the world,"

Roxie said softly. "Just think, if it hadn't been for the Lord Jesus coming into the world, we wouldn't have Christmas."

"Nor happiness or hope, either," Kay continued.

"That's the thing we are so apt to forget, Kay," Carl Orlis said, his voice hushed. "Christ's birthday marks the beginning of hope and happiness for all mankind. All the good things of life come from our Lord Jesus, and the fact that He was born on this earth to bear our sins." He took a deep breath. "But we often get to thinking so much of gifts for our loved ones and let ourselves get so busy at Christmas time doing things that actually aren't very important, that we almost forget that the whole observance of Christmas is to remember Christ's birth."

"That's certainly true," Roxie put in. "I wanted that dress so much that I bought it, and if it hadn't been for Danny and the man who ran the store, I wouldn't have been able to give anyone gifts."

"We all are guilty of things like that, Roxie," Mrs. Orlis said, smiling understandingly. "That doesn't excuse us, of course, but the important thing is for us to realize it when we have done something wrong and make it right."

Roxie Orlis nodded her agreement.

CHAPTER 12

A SHOPLIFTER!

The months passed quickly at school and almost before the young people realized it summer was upon them once more. Kay had a job at the Broken Arrow Bible Camp as swimming instructor in the Lake of the Woods not far from Angle Inlet. At the first opportunity Danny went over to see her.

They sat together during the campfire service, and then walked out to the end of the dock where they talked for a few minutes.

"I'm going to start guiding at Monument Bay in the morning," he told her.

I'm so glad. I've been praying that you would get a job."

He picked up a stone and skipped it across the placid water. "It's tough work, but it's a job."

"What about guiding on Sunday?"

"They know how I stand. That wasn't any problem at all."

They talked for a moment or two longer. Then Danny walked to Kay's cabin with her and went back to his boat. He was just turning it about in the water before starting the motor when he heard something in the darkness. He looked up quickly. There, not a hundred yards away, was the dark shape of a canoe, gliding silently through the reeds toward shore.

Danny crouched in the boat, staring.

What would anyone be doing out with a canoe at that hour? And why would he be stealing up to the Bible Camp? And why would he land over there in the brush instead of at the dock?

Danny crouched tensely in the darkness. One person was in the canoe, but it was too dark to see his features. While Danny waited, the person beached the canoe and disappeared into the brush.

Danny hesitated, then pushed the *Scappoose* back to the dock and told the camp director what he had seen.

"I'll get out the men counselors," Mr. Marlow said, "and we'll give the place a good combing. But to tell you the truth, Danny, I can't figure out why anyone would want to sneak in here. We certainly don't have anything that would be worth stealing."

"I thought of that too. Then it occurred to me that it might be someone who had sneaked out after hours and was just going back. Whoever it was, he acted as though he knew exactly where he was going, and what he was going to do. He certainly didn't waste any time."

"I'll check on that," the director replied, "but I'm sure that the boys are all present and accounted for. We take a careful bed check every night shortly after 'lights out.'"

Danny stayed while they searched the camp, but they found nothing.

"Are you sure that you saw someone?" the camp director asked when they had finished the search.

"I'm positive."

"I can't understand it. I've checked with the counselors. They say that everyone was in when they made their check at 10 o'clock."

"Could someone have left after 10 o'clock?" Danny asked, glancing at his watch. It was almost midnight.

"I suppose that's possible," Mr. Marlow admitted, "but it hardly seems likely. Where would they go at that hour? And what would they do?"

Nevertheless, Danny Orlis was still disturbed about it when he went back home. So disturbed that he awakened Ron and talked with him about it.

"I don't know for sure what's going on over there," he said, "but it's something mighty strange."

"You had just been to see Kay," Ron told him sleepily. "You probably had so much star dust in your eyes that you imagined you were seeing things."

"That's almost what the camp director tried to tell

me," Danny answered. "But I know better. Somebody came to that island by canoe, and whoever it was, he didn't want anyone to see him. He didn't go up to the dock. He paddled ashore near the thickest part of the woods."

"But you said yourself that they didn't find anyone," Ron said. "They didn't even find an extra canoe."

"I know that," Danny said. "But there's something strange going on over there."

"Is there something you want me to do about it?" Ron asked.

"I don't know that there's anything any of us can do."

"Then how about letting me get some sleep?" Ron rolled over and buried his face in his pillow.

Danny Orlis left early the next morning for the resort on Monument Bay.

Two or three nights later he managed to see Kay again.

"Did you hear anything more about the person I saw stealing up to the island in a canoe the other night?" he asked when they were alone.

She shook her head.

"They searched the island again the next day. All the canoes were there, and there weren't any extra ones. Mr. Marlow said that the only thing he could figure out is that the guy heard you and was frightened away."

"But I didn't frighten him," Danny said. "I didn't

even move until after he disappeared into the brush. No, Kay, he went ashore on the island. I know he did."

"To tell you the truth, Danny," she answered, "we've got another problem here at camp that has just about knocked everything else into the background."

"It must be something bad."

"It is," she went on. "Someone has been stealing from the camp book table."

Danny Orlis pursed his lips. "Now that is something for a Christian camp, isn't it?" he said. "Are they sure the stuff is being stolen?"

"They're positive of it," she answered. "At first they only missed a few small things, and no one was particularly alarmed. Mr. Marlow said that sort of thing happens fairly often. But during the last three or four days they've missed some expensive pictures and at least two expensive Bibles. It's really a terrible thing."

Danny ran his fingers through his shock of sandy hair. "I know a lot of the kids who come here aren't Christians," he said, "but I can't understand their stealing at a Bible camp. You'd think they'd have more respect for the things of the Lord, wouldn't you?"

"It's like Mr. Marlow said at our staff meeting this afternoon," Kay said. "We not only have to think about the things that are being stolen. We've got to think about the one who is doing it. If we don't catch him, he might think that he can always get away with it. It could be the thing that might start him on a life of crime. That's why it's so important that we find out who's been stealing from the book table, Danny."

He nodded seriously.

The next time Danny came over to the Bible camp to see Kay, Mr. Marlow called him into his office and closed the door.

"I was talking with Miss Milburn yesterday," he began softly. "I understand that she told you something about the trouble we've been having at our book table."

Danny nodded. "I thought perhaps it had something to do with the person I saw the other night. But what a person like that would be doing with Bibles is more than I would know."

"I thought of that too, until I checked with the people who have been working at the book table. These thefts have been happening during the day. An item will be in stock in the morning and be missing in the afternoon. So we know that it is someone here at camp."

"That makes for a bad situation, doesn't it?"

Mr. Marlow nodded. "Would it be possible for you to help us out at the book table for a few days, Danny?" he asked. "We need someone who can handle the books and keep a close watch at the same time. We've got to catch this person. For his own good."

"I'd like to be able to help you," the Orlis boy said, "but I'm guiding at one of the resorts. I've already promised them that I'd stay on for the balance of the season."

"Do you know of anyone else who could help us? We'd want a Christian, old enough to be dependable, and discreet enough to be quiet about what he is doing."

"I was just thinking about my kid brother, Ron. He's alert and dependable, and I know he could keep his mouth shut. He'd do a good job for you."

Mr. Marlow's forehead creased thoughtfully. "I had hoped to get someone a little older."

"But Ron is in high school," Danny continued, "and he is a good, solid Christian."

"Well," the camp director said, "I would rather have you, but if you can't come, I'll take your word about your brother. If you think he can handle it, we'll give him a chance."

"He'll handle it all right," Danny said, "and do just as good a job as I could. And I know he'll be glad for an opportunity to make a little extra money."

"Have him come to see me tomorrow," the camp director went on. "And tell him not to talk to me about why he's here until we're in my private office. If it got noised around that we have brought someone in to help find who is stealing from us, the person might be scared off."

"You can count on Ron."

He told Ron about the job that evening, and why Mr. Marlow wanted to hire him. The boy was delighted.

"That sounds like a little excitement."

"And you want to remember that you're not to get too interested in those pretty gals over there," Danny warned, joking. "It might be one of them and it could just break your heart to have to put the finger on her."

"Don't judge me by yourself," Ron said airily. "I've got a heart of stone when it comes to duty."

The following morning Ron went over to the Bible camp to talk with Mr. Marlow.

"We don't want any of the kids to suspect anything," the director said. "So, I think it would be best if you went back home for the rest of the day and then came over to work first thing in the morning."

"That's fine with me," Ron told him. He was tingling with excitement.

That afternoon Ron worked frantically so that he could get as much done as possible before going to camp the next morning.

Ron was out in the cabins when the mail boat came in. Carl Orlis sent Roxie to him with a letter.

"I've got something for you, Ronald," she said with a tantalizing smile. "I'll bet you can't guess where it's from."

"Come on," he said, advancing toward her. "It's for me. Give it here."

"Oh, it smells so sweet that I can hardly part with it!" Roxie said, sniffing at the envelope. "I didn't think you would go with a girl who would use scented sta-tionery. She must be gone on you, Ron. Real gone."

"Quit your clowning and hand that letter over."

"I think I should read it first."

"If you don't give me that letter, I'll–."

She held it out to him.

"Aw," he said, glancing at the envelope. "This isn't from a girl. It's from one of the guys."

"What's the matter?" she chided. "Disappointed?"

The following morning Ron did as planned. He got up early and went over to the Bible camp. He got there just in time to open for business.

There was no one around when he started, and he spent the first hour or two getting acquainted with the stock. But when things finally did pick up the customers came in droves. Ron waited on them as quickly as he could, keeping his eyes open all the while for those who were fingering the stock with-out buying.

"I didn't see anyone that I could be sure about," he confided to Kay that evening, "but Mr. Marlow is right about what's happening. I missed two or three items this afternoon."

"That's the way it's been almost every day," she said. "I can't understand it."

"I probably shouldn't say anything about it," Ron said, "but do you know anything about a guy by the name of Dick Bryan, Kay?"

"Dick Bryan?" she echoed. "Everyone at camp

knows him. Why he's one of the strongest Christians here. I've never seen anyone with such a glowing testimony. He's one who is always talking about the Lord."

Ron hesitated.

"Are you sure?" he asked.

"Well, I haven't known him too long, if that's what you mean," Kay said. "And I don't suppose anyone else at camp has known him over a period of time either. But he gives every indication of being an outstanding Christian. He has such a ringing testimony and is always so quick to testify. What makes you ask about him?"

"I probably shouldn't say anything about this, even to you. But Kay, I would have sworn that I saw him pick up a locket and slip it into his pocket this morning."

"Oh, you must be mistaken!" Kay told him quickly. "Dick isn't like that at all. He wouldn't steal anything."

CHAPTER 13

A CLUE

I haven't said a thing to anyone about Dick Bryan except you, Kay," Ron said the next day. "And I don't intend to say anything until I get a lot more evidence than I've got now. It's like I told you. I could be mistaken. But I did see him make a quick movement of some sort when he thought no one was looking. And I'm almost sure he slipped that locket into his pocket."

"I'm glad that you haven't said anything to anyone else, Ron. I believe Mr. Marlow would as soon suspect one of the members of the staff as he would Dick Bryan. Dick has such an outstanding testimony. It seems that almost every time you turn around you see Dick with one of the kids off in a corner talking about spiritual things."

"But why does he hang around the book table all the time?" Ron asked. "He doesn't buy anything.

Still, he's there most of his free time, hanging over one counter and then another, fingering stuff. He's the only one that does that. Nobody else does."

"I know you think you've got reason to suspect him," Kay said, "but that's just circumstantial evidence. If you want to find out what he's like, wait until the campfire service tonight and you'll see what I mean. Dick will be the first or second one up to testify."

Ron did as Kay suggested and stayed for the campfire service. Sure enough, the moment they announced that there would be testimonies Dick got up and spoke. His voice trembled with emotion and tears filled his eyes.

"Did you ever hear a boy with such spiritual depth?" one of the counselors leaned over and whispered to Ron. "Why, there are Christians here who've known the Lord for twenty-five years who don't have a testimony like that."

It did sound very convincing. And yet Ron wondered about Dick. He wondered even more later in the evening as he passed the cabin where Dick Bryan was staying.

"Are you going to slip out again tonight, Dick?" he overheard one of the guys say in hushed tones as he walked beneath the windows.

"I'll wait until they come around for a bed check," Dick said, laughing. "And then you'll see. Any of you guys going with me? We'll take a canoe and go over to that old fort on Magnuson's Island. That should be a real spooky place on a dark night like this."

Ron stood there momentarily, undecided what to do.

Danny had seen someone hurrying back to the island that first night he came over to see Kay. It must have been Dick. Ron went on to the dock and got into his boat. When he got home, he talked with Danny about it.

"It was probably Dick that I saw," Danny agreed, "but he shouldn't have been out running around when he was supposed to be in bed. Those of us who call the Lord Jesus our Savior should be consistent so that others will want to follow Him. But just because Dick was out after hours is no sign that he's the one who has been stealing from the book table."

"I know that," Ron answered, "but it does show that all those fancy words in his testimony aren't what they're cracked up to be. It's enough to make me suspicious."

"We've got to be very careful, Ron," Danny said, "about accusing anyone of anything. And especially another Christian. I've heard Dick give his testimony too. And I'm like Kay. I'd hate to believe that anyone who speaks out as strongly for the Lord as Dick does would stoop to stealing."

That night the two brothers prayed for a long while about it.

The next day, and the next passed without incident. Ron worked hard at the book table and kept his eyes open, but he saw nothing out of the way.

The afternoon of the third day, Dick Bryan came around during a slack period and engaged him in conversation.

"Isn't this camp a wonderful place?" he began. "I feel as though I've been drawn so much closer to the Lord during my stay here. I'm sure thankful that I won the good conduct award. I get to stay another two weeks."

Ron looked at him quizzically. "You won the good conduct award?" he asked before he thought. "How come?"

"The camp gives a good conduct award for the one who obeyed the rules the best and was the best example to the other kids." He spoke with cultivated modesty. "I guess they figured that I was the one who should have it. But I don't know why."

"Neither do I," Ron blurted without thinking.

Dick Bryan's cheeks flushed and for a moment or two he said nothing. Then, "Isn't it terrible about all those things being stolen from the book table?"

Ron Orlis' eyes narrowed. Kay and Mr. Marlow had told him that none of the kids in camp knew about the thefts. Only a few of the staff knew. "Has there been stealing going on here?" Ron asked pointedly.

Dick Bryan's face went white and beads of perspiration dotted his forehead.

"I guess I shouldn't have said anything about it," he said lamely. "But I heard Mr. Marlow talking with one of the staff members last night. He mentioned that some things had been stolen from the book table, and I was horrified. I can't imagine anyone stealing Bibles and pictures and plaques, can you?

"No," Ron answered firmly, "I can't imagine a Christian stealing anything, but especially Bibles and that sort of thing. We can be sure of this, though, a thief is always caught."

Dick Bryan smiled briefly.

"I certainly hope he is," he said. And then he moved away.

There wasn't anything wrong with what Dick had said. And it could be that he had overheard Mr. Marlow discussing the matter with someone on the staff. The camp director was concerned about the thefts and had talked it over with several other people. Yet why should Dick have been the one to overhear him? Somehow it didn't ring true. Dick made a definite point of talking about the Lord, but it seemed to Ron as though he were trying to make a good impression more than anything else. Why? What difference would it matter whether Ron thought that he was deep spiritually?

Ron wanted to talk it over with Kay, but she was busy when he was ready to leave.

On arriving at home, he went straight to his room, and after the usual Bible reading and prayer time Ron decided to get to bed early. What should he do? He could not dismiss the matter from his mind. Later his older brother came into their room.

CHAPTER 14

"A THIEF IS ALWAYS CAUGHT"

When the Orlis boys were in bed that night they lay for a long while talking.

"By the way," Danny said at last, "how are you coming with your detective work over at the camp?"

"I still think Dick Bryan knows more about it than he lets on, or anyone else knows," Ron said. "There's something peculiar about the guy. He seems to have to keep telling everyone what a good Christian he is."

"Maybe he loves the Lord so much that he wants to testify to everybody," Danny said. "I've known guys who are that way. They were outstanding Christians and did a real job of soul winning."

"I've seen guys like that too. But Dick doesn't strike me as being that kind. There's something slick and deceiving about him. He acts as though he wants everyone to believe that he really knows the Lord and is the best Christian in camp. If a guy is really born again, his life should do some of the speaking for him. He shouldn't have to grab every guy he meets and tell him how spiritual he is."

Danny nodded. "I agree with you, Ron. But you want to be very sure that you've got indisputable evidence before you say anything to Mr. Marlow about him or anyone else. It could do a great deal of harm if you had him call in someone only to find him innocent."

"Don't worry. If I don't get good, strong evidence, I'm not going to make any report at all."

"I've been praying a lot about this thing," Danny continued. "And I know that you have too. It isn't just a matter of stopping the stealing. That's serious enough and should be stopped, of course. But this affair goes deeper than that. If whoever is taking these things gets away with it, he's going to get bolder. When he gets back home, the chances are that he'll start taking things from stores, or maybe break into houses. Then he'll be caught and the only thing anyone can do is send him to the reformatory."

"That's exactly what Mr. Marlow told me when I started to work there," Ron said. "He's much more concerned about the one who is taking the things than he is about the loss to the camp."

The following day it happened.

Ron was busy with a customer as Dick Bryan approached the book table from the side. He didn't think that Ron was watching, but the Orlis boy turned just as Dick drew his hand from the table and shoved it slyly into his pocket.

"Dick!" Ron said sharply. So sharply that the boy froze. "What are you doing with that necklace?"

"What necklace?" Dick Bryan echoed, blustering.

"The one you had in your hand," Ron said. "The one you just stuffed into your pocket."

"I didn't put anything into my pocket," Dick answered belligerently. "What are you trying to do? Accuse me of stealing?"

Ron Orlis turned to his assistant. "You take over here," he said. "We're going to see Mr. Marlow."

By this time eight or ten guys and girls about Dick's age had gathered around.

"I'll say we are going to see Mr. Marlow," Dick said, highly indignant. "We're going to see him and get to the bottom of this. I know that Christians are often persecuted, but I certainly didn't think that it would happen in a Bible camp. I didn't think that a guy would be accused of stealing just because he has a good, strong testimony." He turned to Ron. "But you're not going to get away with this!" he went on loudly. "I'll show you that I'm not guilty. You'll be discharged. That's what will happen!"

Ron Orlis could feel the doubtful, questioning stares of the others as he and Dick walked along the path to the director's office. What if he had made a mistake?

Mr. Marlow was at his desk.

"Mr. Marlow," Dick bristled angrily, "Ron Orlis has dragged me here like a common thief. He accused me of stealing from the book table!"

The camp director's eyes widened.

"Are you sure you haven't made a mistake, Ron?" he asked incredulously. "Dick has been a model camper. He even won our good conduct award and was given another two weeks here. You can't be serious."

"I saw him take a necklace from the table," Ron said doggedly, "and put it into his pocket. It isn't the first time, either. There have been two or three other occasions when I thought I saw Dick take something. But today, I am positive."

Mr. Marlow turned to the other boy. "What do you have to say for yourself?"

"If you believe what he's saying, search me," Dick answered. "Go through my pockets and see whether I've got anything in them."

The camp director hesitated.

"Go on!" Dick demanded. "Search me!"

Mr. Marlow went through the boy's pockets carefully. Then he turned to Ron.

"There isn't a thing in any of his pockets that doesn't rightfully belong to him," he said.

"See!" Dick Bryan cried. "What did I tell you?"

Ron felt the color drain from his cheeks. The strength drained from his body, leaving him weak and trembling.

Mr. Marlow laid the contents of Dick Bryan's

pockets on the desk before him. "There isn't a thing here that doesn't belong to Dick," he said.

"See?" the accused boy said, turning to Ron. "What did I tell you? I didn't have a thing to do with that stealing, and I've proved it!"

The camp director turned to Ron. "What have you to say for yourself?" he asked. His voice was hard, almost accusing. "What explanation do you have for bringing Dick here this way?"

"I saw him take that necklace, Mr. Marlow," Ron protested lamely. "Honestly I did."

"Hmm," the camp director pursed his lips tightly. "That's a serious charge. A very serious charge to make against one who has such a ringing Christian testimony."

"I know that," Ron went on desperately. "That's why I didn't make it the first time I suspected him. There have been two or three times in the past few days when I thought I saw Dick slip something into his pocket, but I wasn't sure. Today I know that he took that necklace. I'm positive he did."

Mr. Marlow was silent for almost a minute.

"What do you have to say about this, Dick?"

"You already know the answer to that," Dick said, blustering. "I didn't have anything to do with it. Not a thing. Ron is just jealous of me. That's all. He wants to hurt my testimony."

"Is there anything else that makes you suspect

Dick," the director asked, "aside from the fact that you thought you saw him slip something off the table?"

"Yes, there is. For one thing, he hung around the book table all the time. He didn't buy anything, but every time I turned around, he was there, hanging over the counter, or picking things up and fingering them."

The color came up in Dick's cheeks again.

"I've been going to buy something," he said, "if my parents send me any money. I was trying to pick out gifts for the family – something I could take home with me."

"And another thing, Dick told me how terrible he thought it was that someone would steal from the camp book table. And you told me yourself, Mr. Marlow, that no one knew about the thefts except yourself and two or three staff workers."

"I did not say anything to you about those thefts," Dick blurted. "You're just making that up. You've got it in for me and you're trying to blame me for something I didn't do. You're lying now."

Mr. Marlow got to his feet and crossed to the doorway. "Dick," he began, turning to face the camper, "there's something I think you should know. Ron Orlis came here at my request, not only to work at the book table, but to help us find the person who has been stealing from the book table."

Dick Bryan's face turned pale.

"But I didn't do it," he protested feebly. "I did

overhear you and–and one of the counselors talking about some stuff being stolen. And I–I did mention it to Ron, but I didn't steal anything. I swear that I didn't steal anything."

Mr. Marlow listened to him quietly.

"You realize that you're admitting you just lied to me," he said when the boy had finished speaking, "don't you?"

Dick bit his lower lip but said nothing.

"I don't suppose you would object if we got your suitcase and went through it, would you?" the camp director asked.

"Go through my things?" Dick echoed, his voice taking on a new and wild note. "What do you mean? Can't you believe me when I tell you that I didn't steal anything? Can't you take my word for it?"

"You've just admitted that you told me something that wasn't true. If a boy will lie about one thing, he might lie about something else."

"But you didn't find the necklace in my possession. That should be proof."

"You could have slipped the necklace out of your pocket on your way over here and dropped it along the path or in the brush. Of course, if you have nothing in your suitcase that doesn't belong to you, you won't have a thing to worry about. We're not out to persecute you or to take advantage of you. We'd much rather prove that you were innocent than guilty. Believe me."

"I don't have anything over there that doesn't belong to me," Dick said nervously. "But I just don't like the thought of being searched. You can't search me if I don't want you to."

"I wouldn't go through your things unless you told me that I could," the camp director assured him. "But your refusal would be practically the same as admitting that you are guilty."

Dick hesitated.

By this time, his lips had turned blue and his shoulders were trembling.

"Is it all right for us to send somebody to get your suitcase and bring it here?" Mr. Marlow asked again.

Dick nodded, almost imperceptibly.

He called in one of the counselors and asked him to go down to Dick's cabin.

"Bring the suitcase and anything else that is Dick's here to the office," he directed. "We don't want to go through his things down there where the other boys can see what we are doing."

As soon as the counselor was gone, Dick turned to Mr. Marlow.

"What are you going to do to me?" Dick asked tremulously.

"What do you mean?"

"You–you aren't going to send me to the reformatory, are you?" he asked, his voice pleading. "Somebody else could have put those things in my suitcase. All the guys know where I keep my things. And I don't have a lock on my suitcase. One of them could have put those things in there just for spite."

"Then you do have some stolen property in your suitcase," Mr. Marlow said.

Dick nodded miserably. Ron Orlis turned away. He didn't feel very good about what had happened.

"I–I don't know why I did it," Dick said, his voice quaking. "I really didn't mean to. I wanted something to take home to some of the people I knew and I didn't have money to buy anything."

Mr. Marlow picked up a pencil and turned it in his fingers thoughtfully.

"I'm sorry to hear this, Dick," he said in a quiet and kind voice. "I'm terribly sorry."

Tears welled in the boy's eyes.

"But," Mr. Marlow went on, "I am glad that you've confessed to it."

"W-w-what are you going to do to me?" the boy asked again.

"We'll have to talk that over with the counselors," the camp director answered. "We'll want to talk with you again as soon as we have had a meeting with the staff."

"You–you aren't going to call the sheriff, are you? You aren't going to have him arrest me and–and throw me into jail, are you? You wouldn't do that."

"Go to your cabin, Dick," Mr. Marlow went on. His voice was kind, but firm and insistent. "We'll call you when we are ready to talk with you."

When the boy was gone the camp director turned to Ron.

"I want to thank you, Ron," he said, "for what you did. That boy had me and the rest of the staff completely fooled."

"I guess he would have fooled me too," Ron said, "if I'd known what he was supposed to be before I got suspicious of him."

Mr. Marlow pushed back in his chair. "I can't understand that boy," he said. "From the very first day he came here he had such a glowing testimony. I can't figure him out at all."

"I talked with Kay Milburn and my brother, Danny," Ron said. "They both said that I must have been mistaken in suspecting him. And I thought I was too. But I kept seeing him do things that were suspicious." Ron leaned forward. "It sort of makes a guy sick when someone, who is supposed to have such a strong testimony for the Lord, gets into a mess like this, doesn't it? Do you suppose he really is a Christian?"

Mr. Marlow shook his head.

"It's not for me to say whether or not he's a born again believer," he answered. "That's a matter between Dick and the Lord. But we know this much about it. He certainly hasn't conducted himself as a Christian."

CHAPTER 15

THE RUNAWAY SAVED

When Ron had discovered who had been stealing from the book table his work was done. He collected his check for the days that he had worked and started down to the dock.

Dark, ugly storm clouds had gathered in the west and were boiling over the horizon. It wouldn't be long before the wind would rise and the lake would be lashed with rain. He stood on the dock for two or three minutes watching the clouds. Danny and Dad would probably say that it would be best to wait. But if a storm did come, it could tie him up at the camp for the night. And he'd just as soon be out of there if the story about Dick got out among the kids. He didn't want them slipping up to him and asking questions. He'd like to forget about the whole affair. That's what he really wanted to do.

Ron got into his boat and turned it about to head

out into the bay. He should feel good. They had hired him to take care of the book table and catch the person who had been stealing from it. He should be proud of himself. But he didn't feel that way. He could still see the pale, frightened look on Dick Bryan's face as he confessed, the pain in the boy's eyes. A thing like that was enough to keep anyone from feeling good.

Ron began to pray silently for Dick Bryan, and that everything would work out to the glory of God.

Ron thought there would be time for him to get home before the storm hit, but it was building up faster than he had thought. He was just rounding the tip of Magnuson's Island when the rain and wind hit him hard. He stiffened and squinted out across the bay. Great, white-laced breakers were rising fast.

"Hmm," he said to himself. "I'd better go ashore until this thing blows over."

He was making a wide turn when he caught sight of a canoe, its gleaming, silvery bottom up.

Ron sucked in his breath sharply.

There was someone in the water, clinging desperately to the canoe. And then he saw that the canoe had come from the Broken Arrow Bible Camp. And the boy in the water was Dick Bryan!

Even as Ron brought the boat about and headed for the overturned canoe, he heard a faint cry for help.

"I'm coming!" he shouted above the roar of the wind. "Hang on! I'm coming!"

The waves hit the *Scappoose* broadside and almost

swamped her. Ron cut the speed and pushed her nose into the breakers so that she would ease up over them. Dick didn't seem to be in any particular trouble. It would be better to ease closer to him than to take a chance of capsizing.

"Hang on, Dick!" Ron called again.

Carefully he inched the *Scappoose* in until her nose almost nudged the canoe.

"Now grab hold of this oar!" he ordered.

"I don't know whether I can or not!"

"You've got to!" Ron repeated. "Now take hold of this oar and let me help you ashore."

Reluctantly Dick loosened his grip on the canoe and took hold of the outstretched oar. "Now let me get into the boat," he pleaded, his teeth chattering. "I can't hang on another minute."

"Can't do that," Ron said. "You'll upset us and then we will be in a fix. Here, let me get this anchor rope around you so you won't have to hang on so tight."

"Let me in the boat, Ron," he pleaded. "P-p-please let me in the boat!"

But Ron Orlis did not answer him. Instead, he got the heavy anchor rope about Dick Bryan's shoulders and under his arms, and tied it securely to the boat seat.

"Now we won't have to depend upon your grip, Dick," he said. "We'll be ashore in a couple of minutes."

"Please let me in the boat, Ron," Dick repeated in desperation. "Please!"

Ron put the motor into gear and continued to inch slowly toward Magnuson's Island. Great driving sheets of rain pounded through his clothes and whipped across the foam-laced breakers.

"Are you all right, Dick?" he shouted.

"I–I think so," the boy in the water answered.

In a few more seconds Ron made it to shore. For an instant or two neither he nor Dick moved.

Dick's breath was coming in low, tearing gasps, and his whole body was trembling.

"I–I didn't think I'd last it out, Ron. I thought I was a goner until you came along."

"But what were you doing over here?" Ron asked him. "I thought you were in your cabin."

Dick swallowed hard.

By this time, the boys had beached the boat, tied it securely, and made their way up to the reconstructed building of old Fort St. Charles. Fortunately, it was unlocked, and they went inside.

"But why did you leave the camp?" Ron asked him again.

"Did you hear what Mr. Marlow said?" Dick asked. His voice still reflected his fright. "He–he was going to have a staff meeting and then call me in and–and–I just know that he was going to call the sheriff and have me put in jail. That's what he was going to do. I couldn't stay there, Ron. I had to run away."

"You can't run away from trouble, Dick," Ron told him firmly. "That's one of the things my dad taught me. Besides, Mr. Marlow didn't even mention sending you to jail. All he said was that he was going to have a staff meeting and wanted to talk with you later."

"But that's what he meant. I know that's what he meant."

"Mr. Marlow is very much concerned about you, Dick," Ron told him then. "He wants to do what's best for you, so that you won't ever do a thing like that again."

The other boy did not answer him. He was sitting there cross-legged, shivering, and biting his lower lip.

"I talked with him after you left," Ron Orlis said. "He wants to be just, but he doesn't want to be harsh or cruel."

"I know what he's going to do," the boy kept repeating. "I know what he's going to do."

Ron looked out of the door. The rain was still slamming against the cement wall and running in little rivulets over the rocks. Silently he prayed for help and guidance.

"There's something I want to talk with you about, Dick," he said at last. "Something very important."

His companion looked up at him.

"Have you taken Christ as your Lord and Savior?" Ron asked. "Have you taken Him as the Master of your life?"

"You heard me give my testimony, didn't you?" Dick answered evasively.

Ron nodded.

"But that isn't what I meant," he went on. "It's like Danny told me one time. It's possible for a guy to learn to talk like a Christian, and even to act like one, without honestly taking Christ as his personal Savior."

"I don't get what you're driving at."

"Anyone can learn to use the language that a Christian uses," the Orlis boy explained. "He can learn to give a testimony and to conform in such a way that most people who come in contact with him will think that he's an outstanding Christian. And still he might never have made a decision for the Lord Jesus Christ himself. He might never have recognized that he is a sinner and in need of a Savior. That's what I'm driving at. Are you really born again, Dick? Are you a Christian?"

The other boy hesitated. "I–I've always thought of myself as a Christian," he repeated.

"But are you a born again believer?" Ron insisted. "Have you taken a definite stand for the Lord Jesus Christ? Have you let Him in to be the Master and Lord of your life, or." Ron paused prayerfully. "Or," he repeated, "have you just been using the language of a Christian to try and fool those with whom you've come in contact?"

Dick Bryan flushed under the barbs. "I–I don't think I know what you mean," he stammered.

"Sometimes a guy wants to convince other people that he is a believer," Ron went on softly. "So he gets up and testifies with the best of them. He talks as though he is the most pious person on earth. But if he's only doing it to deceive someone, it doesn't do any good at all. Before your testimony, or mine, can mean anything, we've got to mean business with God."

As Ron Orlis continued to talk, Dick leaned forward intently.

"That–that's just the way I have been, Ron," Dick said at last. "I really didn't want to be. But I wanted to hang on and control my life myself. I wanted to be able to do all the things I wanted to do. I wanted to have fun when I got out on my own."

Ron smiled faintly.

"Now you see what happens when we try to run our lives ourselves," he said. "Things get in a mess. We can't do things the way God wants us to unless we've given our lives over to Him completely. It can't just be lip service."

The other boy nodded.

"You might fool your parents, and all the people at camp, and everyone you meet," Ron went on, "but you can't fool the Lord Jesus. He knows what's in the heart." Ron hesitated, waiting for his words to sink home. "Maybe that's why God permitted this thing to happen. So that you'll know how weak and foolish you really are. How weak and foolish we all are unless we have put our trust in Him."

Dick looked away and mopped the tears that filled his eyes.

"Do you suppose God could–could take me after what I've done?" he asked.

"Jesus said, 'The one who comes to Me I will certainly not cast out,'" Ron said softly. "In the Lord's eyes the big sin is rejection. And you don't have to reject Him any longer. You can settle that right now."

Together the boys got down on their knees and prayed.

* * *

When the storm was finally over, Ron and Dick went out in the boat, lashed the canoe securely to one side, and went back to the Bible camp.

"W-w-would you go with me to talk with Mr. Marlow, Ron?" Dick asked as they neared shore.

"Of course," the Orlis boy answered.

Somebody told the camp director that the boat was coming and he went down to the dock to meet it. So did half the staff and kids at camp.

"I want to tell you how sorry I am for what I did," Dick began abruptly, looking straight into Mr. Marlow's eyes. "And I want to make things right."

The director looked around at the crowd that had gathered about them.

"Don't you think it would be better to go to my office, Dick?" he asked. "We can discuss the matter privately there."

The boy was silent momentarily.

"I–I'd like to," he said, stammering. "But I'd like to have everybody hear what I've got to say too. I did what I did because I didn't really know the Lord Jesus Christ as my personal Savior. I was just one of those kids who conformed, who tried to sound as though he were a believer."

An excited little ripple went through the crowd that was standing there.

"I guess that's why I felt I had to testify all the time," he continued, "to keep reminding people that I was a Christian. I don't want you to think that all the guys and girls who get up to testify are like that, because they're not. The trouble was that my testimony was just empty words. I hadn't really experienced those things deep down in my heart."

Mr. Marlow started to speak during the long silence, but Dick went on.

"I don't know how many of you know about it, but I was the one who stole from the book table."

Tears welled in his eyes.

A gasp went up from the crowd.

"It was a terrible, wicked thing to do," Dick continued. "I want you all to forgive me. You see, I took the Lord Jesus as my Savior this afternoon. For the first time in my life, I am a Christian!"

Ron Orlis moved closer to Dick and put his arm about the younger boy's trembling shoulder.

THE DANNY ORLIS SERIES

The Danny Orlis series, by Bernard Palmer, delivers a blend of adventure, mystery, and suspense through various settings—from the Canadian wilderness to Guatemalan jungles. Danny Orlis, an adept outdoorsman, skilled athlete, and committed Christian, employs his quick thinking, calm bravery, and biblical solutions to confront everyday problems and hair-raising dangers. Early stories focus on Danny navigating school life, sports, and outdoor challenges, while in later books, Danny and his wife Kay provide wisdom and guidance to youngsters facing lifelike situations and challenges. Having sold over two million copies, this series has made Palmer a renowned author in Christian youth literature. Palmer is also the author of the Felicia Cartright series and various other series for Christian youth.

AVAILABLE FROM WWW.ANEKOPRESS.COM

www.ingramcontent.com/pod-product-compliance
Lightning Source LLC
Chambersburg PA
CBHW070658100726
47907CB00007B/2262